I0570412

THE ITALIAN JOB

A Contemporary Romance

by

Phyllis A. Humphrey

Published by Criterion House
Printed by CreateSpace

ISBN:978-1-884162-41-1

DEDICATION

To my wonderful husband, who is not only my computer guru, graphics designer and constant supporter, but also takes me to glamourous places which I can write about in my books.

ACKNOWLEDGMENTS

Many thanks to my critique partners, Hilary, Eileen, Gail, Marsha and Jim.

Chapter 1

I landed the assignment to go to Rome—not because I was the best writer on the staff of *L. A. Life Magazine*, nor because I could speak Italian, (because I couldn't). My incredibly important skill was availability. Time was short, Jason was on his honeymoon, Pamela was very pregnant. And no less than three staff members were out with the flu, or so they said. In May, go figure. Or perhaps it was because no one else was willing to fly over 6,000 miles on two-days' notice. Shows what a stunningly bad social life can do for you.

Even so, my boss, Mr. Hardcastle, the first part of whose name should give you an idea of his personality, hesitated long enough before giving his assent to grow mold on my sweaty palms.

"You aren't going to mess up again, are you?"

Like I planned to. Like climbing into the window of a strange person's hotel room on my previous assignment for the magazine had been a well-thought-out decision. In truth, it was nothing but a fluke, the unavoidable result of making a serious miscalculation. Which, I fervently vowed, would never happen again.

"No, of course not." I straightened up to my full five feet, six inches and shook my head. Which unfortunately set my ponytail swinging, not a good thing.

Hardcastle frowned. "So go already. My secretary will give you the tickets and itinerary. Take your laptop and be sure it works this time."

I'd only made that mistake once so he had no call to remind me. And anyway, even without the laptop, I'd remembered almost the entire interview from that assignment and my article was highly praised in some circles.

"And, Sydney, don't forget this is your last chance."

He meant that threat, so I smiled and hurried from his office before he could change his mind about Rome.

The next day I found my never-used passport, had my hair trimmed, and packed my itinerary, tickets and laptop. I planned to record every minute of my first European experience into my journal and tucked it into my seriously overpriced handbag. I went to bed before nine in order to catch a very early flight out of Los Angeles the next morning.

However, as so often happens with me, I couldn't fall asleep for hours. My brain wanted to replay the episode of the window, perhaps to reinforce in my conscious mind that the entire thing had not been my fault.

I'd been given the assignment to interview a minor local politician running for office in the next election, and I sat opposite him in an armless chair in his hotel room. I asked questions and he answered politely but softly in what I later realized he considered a sexy voice. As I leaned forward to hear him, my skirt hiked up over my knees. I attempted to pull it down, dropped my notebook and bent to pick it up, and suddenly he was all over me like a case of hives.

I managed to get out of his clutches and protested in no uncertain terms, but he would have none of it. We did a little cha-cha around the sofa, and then, after slowing him down by pushing an end table in front of him, I grabbed my purse, dashed into the bedroom, and slammed the door.

Yes, that might sound like a foolish thing to have done, but I knew that old hotel. The windows were actually French doors and led to outside balconies. My aim was to get out there and call for help.

Much to my surprise, he didn't follow me. Maybe he had a phone call, or he fell over the end table, or someone came to the door, but my problem remained. It was dark—he had set the interview time for evening—and the balcony was two stories above the street, too far for jumping, even if I were an Olympic athlete instead of someone whose only exercise is changing the sheets on her bed.

However, the next balcony being merely a foot away, I decided to swing over to it, enter the next room by way of *those* French doors and return to the hotel hallway. The next room, which I could only see through a crack in the closed drapes, seemed dark and empty. I paused but reasoned that even if someone were staying there, chances were slim it would be another man bent on hanky-panky.

So I hiked up my skirt, swung my legs over the two balcony railings and gently tried the handle of the door. It was jerked open from inside, and suddenly I was face to face with a fledgling actor who was in town to audition for a part in an upcoming film.

Of course, I didn't know his occupation at the time. That came in the next-day's newspapers. Even so, it could all have ended unobtrusively except that someone had apparently called a *paparazzo*, who flashed a bright light at me. I froze like a safe-cracker with his hand on the dial, Mr. Actor pulled me into his room, and I found myself among a dozen people watching a film clip on the room's DVD player.

I was labeled a "groupie," handed an eight-by-ten glossy signed by the actor, and laughingly sent on my way.

Except that, someone had taken pictures, and, as a result of the sudden publicity, Mr. Actor got a role in an action-adventure film. At the same time, while climbing over the balcony, my handbag had slipped off my shoulder, and the photographer found the magazine's business cards. Mr. Hardcastle was not amused.

I wrote up the interview as if none of that had occurred, because I preferred to think the politician, perhaps, had never behaved that way before. Also, I learned a long time ago that I have plenty of faults of my own, so I lean toward forgiving others for theirs.

* * *

Sydney's Journal

Day One

I flew from Los Angeles to Washington several hours later than I expected to. Some of the first class seats had developed problems requiring the ministrations of a maintenance crew, and we were unable to board for some time. As usual, my luck had decided not to be a lady that day. The airline generously offered us coupons for Starbucks coffee while we waited. Nevertheless, I missed my connecting flight, and evening arrived before I landed in Washington, boarded a Boeing 747 to Rome and plopped into a window seat in coach.

Almost immediately after stowing my suitcase in the overhead bin and tucking my laptop and purse under the seat in front of me, I realized the man standing in the aisle spoke to my seat-mate in French. I couldn't speak Italian, but I had studied French in school and mentally translated, *"Vous ete Francais?"* to mean, "You are French?"

Having received a *"Oui,"* in response, the man, who was slender, sandy-haired, and dressed casually in khaki pants and a knit pullover, spoke again to the man currently sitting in the aisle seat next to me.

"Voulez-vous desire a changez avec moi?" Sandy-hair accompanied the question with gestures, pointing first to the seat the Frenchman occupied and then to the one in the center five-seat row ahead.

The Frenchman bobbed his head, said, *"Merci,"* and immediately retrieved a brown tote-bag from in front of his feet and rose to make the switch.

After which, Sandy-hair dropped into the just-vacated seat next to me and stowed his own bag. He turned to me and, as if he felt the need to explain, said, in American English that he'd obviously grown up speaking, "He's traveling with his wife and daughter, and I thought they'd prefer to sit together."

"How very nice of you." I smiled briefly and turned toward the window, where my vision took in only the sight of the stubbornly-unmoving jetway.

Sandy-hair seemed compelled to offer more explanation. "I noticed they didn't have seats together in the first place. Maybe they booked late or, like me, they prefer the bulkhead row and couldn't get three seats together."

I thought his earnest speech made some reply necessary. "But now you've given up your own seat in the bulkhead row."

He grinned. "It seemed like a good idea at the time. He looked as if he were embarrassed that his generosity had been noted, and I admired that. I also found him quite good-looking and younger than I first thought, maybe early thirties or even late twenties.

He was also quite tall, which made his giving up his seat even kinder. "I suppose you like the extra leg room?"

"Plus the fact there'd be no one sitting in front of me to put the back of his seat down in my lap."

"I know what you mean." I smiled in sympathy, although I hadn't done as much traveling by air as this man apparently had.

"It can be claustrophobic. These coach seats are narrow to begin with, and when that happens I feel as if I'm sitting in a coffin." He shrugged as if he'd survived worse.

I felt rapport building but then checked myself. I

was not there to get acquainted with a good-looking man. Hardcastle meant it when he said the assignment might be my last. I mustn't blow it.

"Do you speak French?" Sandy-hair asked next.

"*Un petite peu.*" I put my forefinger and thumb together, like holding a pinch of salt.

He grinned again, a really sincere, friendly grin. "In France perhaps?"

"No, in high school about a thousand years ago."

"If you're like me, a hundred anyway. Do you also know a wee bit of Italian?"

"Unfortunately no." I liked his looks, his smile and his courtesy, but what I didn't need just then was a long conversation to distract me from what my boss expected me to do. I was rescued from having to say more because the flight attendant came through the aisle reminding us to fasten our seatbelts. The jumbo jet began to move.

"That's too bad. It's seven hours to Rome, and I have an English-to-Italian dictionary in my bag. Would you like to borrow it?"

"Thanks, but I have to read this." I held up the guidebook of Rome, Florence and Venice I had promised Hardcastle I'd read on the flight.

He held up a paperback mystery, one of those modern ones where the women practice karate as well as they pronounce it.

I didn't comment, and he nodded and turned aside, as if assuming I'd rather not be disturbed. That was the message I needed to send, although I was regretting it every second.

While the plane taxied to the runway and finally

took off, I thought of what my mother always said when she knew I was headed out on a traveling assignment: that a single woman traveling alone had better be prepared to be hit on by men. As if I didn't know. In my twenty-five years I'd had enough encounters with men to know that some did, and usually not because they expected me to be the most witty and erudite of companions. Besides, the memory of the incident with the politician remained only too fresh in my thoughts. He definitely had something else on his mind than wondering if I shopped on Rodeo Drive. However, I hadn't expected to fend off a male so soon on that trip. I thought I might have to wait until I got to Italy where they allegedly pinched women's bottoms as a matter of culture.

I didn't really feel this particular man had behaved at all aggressively, especially considering we were to be seat-mates for seven hours. A little polite conversation undoubtedly went with the territory. In fact, keeping unsuitable men from trying to seduce me often made sticking strictly to business on assignments a sizeable chore. I sometimes considered myself a misfit: a prudent woman in the new millennium when Americans were allowed, if not obliged, to be hedonistic.

The flight attendant appeared again and took drink orders. I asked for Seven-Up, then put my book in my lap and lowered the tray table so she could put a package of nuts and a paper napkin on it. My companion did the same, and I noticed he'd ordered Seven-Up as well. I couldn't help smiling at that. At least he didn't plan to get drunk during the flight.

The smile must have done it. He offered his hand. "I'm Taylor Mitchell. If I'm bothering you, just tell me to shut up."

I would never do that, even with Hardcastle's threats running around like gerbils in my head. Besides, since it would be hard to ignore someone seated so close to me during the long flight—I didn't sit that close to a date in a movie theatre—I thought we might as well be friendly.

I put out my own hand. "Sydney Cooke."

"I gather you're traveling alone. Business or pleasure?"

"Business. I'm researching an article for the magazine I work for. How about you?"

"I'm on vacation, using my frequent flyer miles. I missed a flight because my program apparently has more blackout days than a punch-drunk boxer."

I liked his sense of humor. Yet before I could answer, the flight attendant reappeared and pushed a cart down the aisle. She asked what we'd like for dinner.

While we ate, he continued the conversation. "After a day or two in Rome, I'm going to Lake Como to paint."

"As in pictures? You're an artist?"

"Part-time. It's more of a hobby, really. In winter I free-lance in computers and electronics, and in spring and summer I paint and sell my work in galleries in Scottsdale and San Francisco."

"Are you famous? Should I have heard of you?" Although impressed, I thought him too young to be famous. However, as a person who knows next to nothing about serious art, I wouldn't know anyway.

He threw back his head and laughed, a rich, throaty sound. "Good heavens, no. It's a nice dream, but I'm not that ambitious. I just like to make enough money to support my life-style. I'm somewhat of a loner."

I assumed his comment, and the fact he wore no wedding ring, meant he wasn't married. Not that I considered him an eligible man. I hoped to meet one sometime, just not now when my job was probably at stake. Still, I liked the fact he wasn't one of those married men who apparently justified an extra-marital fling as long as he left his wife behind in a different zip-code. And then, once the plane landed, I'd probably never see Mr. Mitchell again.

"Did you bring your paints and an easel with you on this trip?"

"Too much hassle and not necessary anymore." He bent down, unzipped his black nylon carryall, and pulled out a camera. "Digital." He offered it to me. "I can take as many as six hundred pictures and store them on tiny discs. Then when I get back home I put them into my computer, print out larger versions and paint from them in my studio."

While I turned the small camera over in my hands, he joked, "Ain't technology wonderful?" Although I knew how they worked because I owned a small digital camera myself, I didn't admit it. I could tell he liked telling me about it. Or else it was an excuse to take my picture and up the stakes.

"Let me show you." He took the camera from me, leaned back into the aisle a little way and pointed it at my face. He clicked a button on the camera and returned it to me.

I saw myself in the tiny screen and handed it back to him. "So now you can erase it and take a picture of something else?"

"I could, but maybe I want to keep this one. In case I ever want to paint a beautiful redhead."

Although I'd been called that before, I think my hair is more brown than red. Yet who am I to disagree with someone who puts "beautiful" in front of it? I felt my face grow warm. I'd had my share of compliments, but somehow I enjoyed this one more than the others.

We talked of weather and the unique problems connected with travel. I felt an attraction toward him growing. We both remembered a smattering of high school French, and although I enjoyed Taylor's company, I kept thinking about the guidebook I should be reading. Then I rationalized almost immediately that Hardcastle surely didn't expect me to study instead of eat. I told myself I'd open the book as soon as the dinner service was over.

When coffee was served and the in-flight movie came on, Taylor looked up at the screen and sighed. "I'm afraid I've seen this before."

"Me too." I made a face. "And wish I hadn't."

He turned to me with a questioning look. "What didn't you like about it?"

I groaned. "Oh, there I go putting my foot in my mouth again." In my opinion, conversation would be more fun if people said what they thought. But, because I often do, I'm unfit for polite society. "I suppose you're going to say you loved it."

"I wondered if you found it as childish as I did."

"I guess ninety percent of movies these days are made for teens."

"The girl in the film was pretty, but, well—"

I'd been thinking, "smart as a smoked salmon," but instead I offered, "Intellectually challenged?"

"How about dumb as a post?"

I laughed. "Close enough."

"I suppose if we're not going to watch the movie we can talk a bit more."

I wanted to, but Hardcastle's voice in my head kept saying, "No, no, no." How was I ever going to study my guidebook at that rate? I pulled the book from under the napkin in my lap and showed it to him again. "I'm supposed to be learning this."

Taylor shrugged. "I guess I ought to try to get some rest. It'll be morning when we land." He pushed his seat back down, turned off his overhead light and closed his eyes. "See you in Rome."

I hoped I hadn't offended him, but he picked the wrong moment to enter my life. I needed my job, and that required I know something about Italy before I got there. I opened the book to the section on ancient Rome. However, due to remembering the window fiasco, I'd had very little sleep the night before, and soon my vision began to blur and I found myself yawning between every sentence I read. Maybe if I just rested my eyes for a few minutes...

Chapter 2

Day Two

I woke to hear the flight attendant ask if I wanted orange juice. I jerked my head up and realized it had been resting on Taylor's pillow instead of mine. In fact, sometime during the night, he must have raised the arm rest between the two seats because I found myself way too close to him, his blanket over mine.

Embarrassed, I pulled myself erect. I straightened up so fast I bumped the seat in front of me hard enough to wake up the chubby businessman who sat there. If he wasn't already awake. I leaned over the seat. "Sorry."

I repeated it to Taylor. "I didn't mean to fall asleep on your shoulder."

"No problem."

I gulped down the orange juice, unfastened my seatbelt, and bent into a nutcracker to retrieve my purse under the chubby businessman's seat. I muttered excuses again and tried to rise. Let's face it, one cannot stand straight when the passenger in the row ahead lowers his seat back. Legs tend not to bend that way. As I started to squeeze past Taylor, he graciously got up and waited in the aisle.

In the plane's lavatory mirror, I discovered my face so adorned with creases I resembled the "Before" shots on Extreme Makeover. I washed my face anyway, brushed my teeth, and reapplied make-up. Next I passed a comb over my head, grateful that my auburn hair had a natural wave that needed no pampering. I didn't always appreciate that fact. Current Hollywood stars wore their hair long and straight. My hair, by contrast, would require an industrial-sized tube of gel before it could do that. Plus, traveling—to say nothing of Mr. Hardcastle's old-fashioned ideas of what women employees should look like—made that impossible anyway.

When I returned to my seat, I found Taylor was gone, having first put our seat backs in the upright position, pulled down the arm rest, and stored both our blankets and pillows under the seats. Once again, he'd been considerate. On the other hand, I'd been trying to discourage him but ended up with my head on his pillow. What kind of message did that send?

By the time he returned, the flight attendant was busily passing out coffee, tea and croissants, and conversation seemed unnecessary. However, I knew I ought to say something.

"I'm so sorry. I didn't mean to fall asleep on your shoulder last night."

Taylor gave me one of his killer smiles. "You didn't bother me a bit. I'm glad you got some rest."

I took a swallow of coffee and wondered what else to say.

He solved the problem for me. "Last night you mentioned you're writing an article for the magazine you work for."

I took a deep breath. "Yes. It's called *L. A. Life,* and

I usually write articles about what's going on in town. This time I'm on an assignment to get a story about a particular tour of Rome, Florence and Venice."

"In that case, I suppose you've traveled a lot."

"Not really. Until now, I stayed in the U.S. Most of my assignments involved automobile travel, out of the way places, things like that."

"So how come a magazine about Los Angeles wants to do a story about a tour of Italy?"

"Our readers are interested in everything." I gave him a laundry list of subjects. "Politics, the entertainment industry, of course, because of Hollywood, but also the environment, business, gardening, health and fitness."

"You forgot travel."

"And we don't just travel around California. The magazine does a foreign travel article at least once a year, sometimes more often."

"Have you been to Italy before?"

"No, I haven't."

"What made them give you this job then? You said you don't speak Italian." He snapped his fingers. "I've got it. You must be a terrific writer."

I couldn't bring myself to tell him the real reason, so I hedged. "I thought I needed a longer trip, something totally absorbing." Like I had a choice of assignments. "Plus I'm single and have no one to hurry home to."

I scolded myself for telling him that, although he'd probably already noticed my own lack of a wedding ring. Besides, it didn't matter, because I'd probably never see him again.

"Well, I for one am glad you're on this flight." Taylor touched my arm for a moment. "I enjoyed our conversation last night."

My face felt warm. Why didn't I meet men like that in L.A. on a dull weekend? I changed the subject. "At least, I'm not driving long distances in a car this time."

"Don't you like to drive?"

"Not in Los Angeles. Traffic is horrendous, but I'm getting used to it. You can't buy a carton of milk in L.A. without getting in a car."

"So tell me about this tour you're writing about."

"It's a very small tour, only ten people and a guide. We go in a van, not one of those huge buses, excuse me, *motor coaches.*"

"What a great idea. Why haven't I heard of it before? I thought in order to see Europe you had to join forty-five other people and follow a fat woman waving an umbrella."

I grinned at the mental picture he'd given me.

"And have your luggage in the hotel lobby by six a.m. to go to the next city."

"You mean like, 'If this is Tuesday, it must be Belgium'?" I remembered an old movie I'd seen on late-night television.

"Exactly. I did that once. We got rousted out of bed at six every morning to board the bus by seven. One morning a guy said to me, 'I didn't know I'd see so many sunrises.'"

I had to laugh. "I'm sure it's more affordable that way. Seeing Europe with a crowd around you is probably better than not seeing it at all."

"I suppose you're right."

"I should talk. If it weren't for this assignment, I might never see Europe myself."

He tried to cross his long legs between the seats but gave up. "I thought one had no choices other than a jumbo bus or a do-it-yourself expedition. I once took one of the former, which can only be described as traveling in close quarters with forty-five of your worst enemies. Since then, I've been traveling alone."

"You don't enjoy that?"

"Yes, but I miss a lot, not having a guide point out the sights and tell me more than I wanted to know about them."

I laughed. "But the guidebooks tell you what to see, and I understand that most museums have audio cassettes you can rent."

"I guess I want more personal attention. Ten people sounds a lot better than forty-five. How does one get on a tour like yours? Could I join it?"

He wanted to join my tour? Was that good or bad? I let my common sense kick in, because it would never happen. "You have to sign up well in advance. Probably there's no room on this one." I rummaged in my handbag and found a card which I handed to him. "Maybe you could sign up for one next year."

He frowned. "What if I want to go now?"

"Well, then, I think you're out of luck."

"When and where does it start? You said you wanted to get to Rome a day early."

"I think it's too late now. We meet at the hotel on Thursday morning."

"I'll be there. Maybe they'll have room for one

more. It can't hurt to ask." He gave me a boyish grin.

I stared at him for awhile. Like my boss, he apparently made quick decisions. Hardcastle once admitted that not all of his had been right, but that the quick ones worked out at least as often as those he mulled over for several days. Then there was me. I tended to think too long before making important decisions, at least when I had enough time to think. And then made wrong decisions anyway.

I frowned. "I'm afraid it would be a waste of time. With only ten openings, it's sure to be filled. Besides, I thought you were anxious to get to Lake Como to paint."

"I planned to spend a week in Rome anyway, so I'll just phone the Grand Imperiale Hotel and say I'll be arriving later. How many days is your tour?"

"Three in each city."

"Even if there's no room for me, can't we spend some time together in Rome?"

My stomach tightened. I'd been far too cozy, albeit unintentionally, with a man I thought I'd never see again. Now he wanted to spend time with me in Rome. Plus he might become a member of my tour and be at my side for the next eleven days. Instead of talking to him, perhaps I should have read my book after all.

Yet, I didn't regret talking to him at all. I realized I wanted to see him again. How often does one meet such a nice person? He had a good sense of humor, and his easy manner made me consider him more like an old school chum than a stranger. Plus we both missed our original flight and disliked the same movie. Good vibes were mounting up.

I gave him a smile and tried to think of the right thing to do. I decided I could at least be polite, so I told Taylor the name of the hotel and the tour guide. Then the plane landed, the passengers erupted into the aisles, reclaimed their carry-ons from the overhead bins and headed for the exits.

Taylor turned back to me. "See you later."

* * *

Somewhere between the plane and customs, I lost sight of him. After stopping at a kiosk to exchange some dollars for Euros, I finally left the terminal and got into a waiting taxi.

The driver sped off as if practicing for *Le Mans*, racing up narrow streets and dodging other taxis, motor-scooters, cars and pedestrians. I clung to the arm rest to keep from crashing from one side to the other, wondering if he got points if he pounded me into veal scallopini.

Then a stop light turned red, he came to a heart-stopping halt, and I almost landed on the floor. I imagined Rome must have a million accidents a year. Yet, I realized the driver had never sounded his horn, nor had any other driver. Now that was a decided difference from American cities.

Rome had plenty of other traffic sounds, but, when I could concentrate on the scene outside, what I found most intriguing were the narrow streets all lined with parked cars. One vehicle could barely get between them, much less two pass each other. Although skillful, the driver's maneuvering nevertheless made me as nervous as a child in an amusement park ride, and I pulled my gaze from the view in front to stare out the side window at the buildings that lined the narrow streets.

They were so different from those in American cities. No skyscrapers. Most seemed only five or six stories high and didn't resemble plain giant boxes as so many did in Los Angeles. They had crenellations at roof lines, decorations over the windows and doors, window boxes. Flowers.

I wanted to write to the L.A. Chamber of Commerce and say, "Why don't we have buildings like this?" No wonder Americans go to Europe for lovely scenery. At home we tear down everything old, beautiful or not, and erect parking buildings.

Before I could drool all over the side window, the taxi made a sharp turn and stopped abruptly in front of an ancient hotel with an aging uniformed doorman and modern brass luggage carriers. I climbed out of the taxi and undoubtedly gave the driver more Euros than he deserved.

The outside of the hotel screamed nineteenth century, but the inside had been brought into the twenty-first with a row of sleek telephones on a side table and computers behind the check-in desk. A middle-aged man, whose badge identified him as the assistant manager, spoke excellent English and welcomed me with a broad smile. Then I rode up to my room in an elevator that reminded me of the one Audrey Hepburn used in that old movie, *Charade*. It consisted of a metal cage that lived inside a curving staircase and required the occupant to close two sets of doors manually.

My large room boasted a king-sized bed covered with a dark-red brocade spread, walls of red silk, floors that I assumed were marble, and a twelve-foot-high ceiling that still showed a faded pattern of leaves, vines and flowers. Perhaps eighteenth century? Then, through an adjoining door, I saw a modern bathroom and my first bidet.

Back in the bedroom, I decided I liked the way Italians lived and wished I could become a native. Actually, I reasoned almost immediately, most Italians probably didn't live any differently than Americans of the same social status, even if their homes or apartments seemed fancier on the outside.

With four children, my middle-class parents hadn't been able to afford a grand house. We lived in a stucco box with three bedrooms and two baths, a standard design in our area. My two brothers shared one bedroom and my sister and I shared another. We did no more squabbling than normal families, went to church on Sunday, took piano lessons, played school sports and generally lived like everybody else.

I'd always liked studying and especially reading, and I knew from a young age that I'd have to save my baby-sitting earnings and birthday money to go to college, even with student loans. I wanted to be a writer, preferably work for a big newspaper. I planned to cover important stories all over the world and win a Pulitzer Prize for journalism.

Okay, so *L. A. Life*, a small local magazine, wasn't exactly *The Los Angeles Times*, but it was a start. And thanks to Mr. Hardcastle inheriting a lot of money along with his dream of becoming a publisher, I had already caught my first foreign assignment. I gazed at my surroundings and relished the moment.

I hung some clothes in the dark walnut wardrobe, put others in the drawers of the matching chest, and pulled on my nightgown. I threw back the bedspread and blanket and slipped between smooth white sheets. Although only noon, I barely had time to close my eyes before I was asleep.

In my dream, I stood behind an airline counter where I told passengers, over and over, that on Wednesday the Paradise Airline and Storm Door Company only went to Budapest, with a stop in Atlanta. After I argued with the passengers, Taylor appeared and proceeded to chase me around the streets of Rome dodging taxis, but he never caught me.

Chapter 3

I woke to a dim room and street sounds coming from open windows, which were swathed in silky, beige curtains. People hurried about on the street below, and my watch face showed it to be late afternoon. In spite of the silly dream, my much-needed nap had refreshed me, and I realized, except for that, and dozing on the plane for a few hours, I'd been up since four-thirty the previous morning.

I didn't live alone. I had a roommate. Nora, a few years older, and way serious, was a good friend, always listening to my screw-ups with sympathy. She was also quiet, clean, and full of interesting trivia from a reading habit that would impress Alex Trebek on *Jeopardy*. Her only quirk seemed to be occasionally buying a few goldfish and a bowl containing little plastic trees and rocks, the very things found in natural fish ponds, right? However, the fish—during their brief lives in her care—were quiet too, and I never had to feed them or change their water.

Not wanting to wake Nora when I left the apartment on Sunday morning, I didn't go into the kitchen and fix any breakfast for myself, not even coffee. I remembered I'd run out of my own favorite brand, and Nora liked hers strong enough to revive a corpse. As for breakfast, although I often thought all meals should be catered by Ben and Jerry, I thought it inappropriate at that hour. Then my stomach reminded me that, although Taylor and I had dinner on the flight from Washington, I'd had nothing to eat after that except for the croissant that morning.

The air from the open window also told me the weather was warm, so I dressed in green silk slacks and a print blouse, tied a sweater around my waist and set out to find food. Once more using the charming old-fashioned elevator, I descended to the lobby and headed for the hotel restaurant. I paused outside its glass-paned doors, but saw no *maitre* d' or any customers in the dining room. What happened to all the people who'd been in the lobby when I checked in? Did they all know something I didn't?

While I wondered how I could get a meal, a familiar voice came from behind me, and I turned to see Taylor Mitchell. So we met again, after all.

"They don't open until seven-thirty. I checked. I could eat a bear, myself." He, too, had changed clothes, and was now wearing an open-necked blue shirt with his khakis.

"Seven-thirty? That's a little late, isn't it?"

"Not in Italy. Some restaurants don't open for dinner until eight."

I sighed. "I suppose we Americans are spoiled, being able to eat at any time of the day or night."

"Where's a Burger King when you need one?" he joked.

I grinned. "I guess I'll have to wait then and hope my stomach doesn't growl loud enough to disturb the natives." I turned to leave, but Taylor stopped me.

"By the way, thanks for the information about your

tour. They had a cancellation, so I'm in."

His announcement made me both happy and uneasy. On one hand, I looked forward to enjoying his company, but on the other, I hoped he didn't think our meeting on the plane gave him some special connection to me. I hadn't meant to fall asleep on his shoulder. Perhaps, unlike the one I'd just had during my nap, I'd been dreaming that time of something romantic. I read romance novels—so sue me.

"I guess that explains your being in this hotel."

"Yes, I thought it would be more convenient."

"Well, I guess I'll see you tomorrow." I gave him a smile and moved toward the open lobby door.

He caught up with me. "May I make a suggestion? I know a fine restaurant near the Trevi Fountain, so we could go there first to kill time before dinner. That is, in case you want to see the fountain. And, also that you'd be willing to have dinner with me."

I didn't answer for a moment, and he continued. "If I'm being too forward, I'm sorry. You won't offend me if you say no. As I said earlier, you can just tell me to go away."

Well, hardly. Sure, I could get rid of him for the moment, but since he had joined my tour, "go away" would not be a viable option in the future.

So I hesitated again, not wanting to either hurt his feelings or send the wrong message. But all those warnings my mother gave me about picking up strange men in foreign places crept into my mind. Yet, to be fair, Taylor was no longer a complete stranger. In spite of trying to fend him off in favor of reading my guidebook, I had begun to like him. A lot.

I thought about something else. Having dinner on board with all those passengers and crew around was one thing, but dining alone with him might give him the wrong idea. He'd been accepted on my tour, or so he said, but was that the truth? So we'd be together for another ten days, and I didn't want him to think we were... what? I needed time to sort that out.

And then I recalled my hunger pangs. Could I wait much longer for food? The rumbling in my stomach told me I had an appetite for anything dead or seriously slowed down.

I looked down for a moment and then into his eyes. "I'm sorry. If you don't mind, I'll just stroll through the city on my own for a while. Perhaps I'll find a pub or some place where I can get a bite to eat. If not, well, I guess I'll be back."

He accepted my decline with a shrug of broad shoulders and a wistful smile. I started off down the sidewalk, and he called after me, "Don't get lost."

"I won't." I turned left at the first corner. I decided to walk until I found an open restaurant, and, should that not work out in a reasonable length of time, return, as I'd hinted to Taylor, to the hotel dining room, which might be open by that time. In any event, I intended to be back before dark.

Pleased with the balmy weather, I strode off, my gaze often straying upward to admire the buildings, most, apparently, apartments, with their old-world architecture, decorative scrollwork and balconies with flowerpots. I turned a corner, saw more lighted shop windows, and hoped I might find a cafe of some kind among them. Yet when I reached the area I saw they were merely shops selling clothing and shoes. Noticing the sky had begun to darken already, I walked more quickly.

Another turn produced more lighted windows, but those were businesses too and were closed for the night. In the next block I again found apartments, and in the street after that I saw several large structures that I decided resembled government office buildings.

Maybe this do-it-alone approach had not been such a good idea. I should have accepted Taylor's offer. I wished I had a map. When I exchanged my money in the terminal earlier, I had seen a display of local maps, and had even picked one up and unfolded it briefly. As large as a bedspread, it had tiny print and a million pastel-colored squares. A lot of good that would do me. I wouldn't know the name of any of the streets. So I had attempted to refold it, gave up and stuffed it back in the rack. I didn't need it. I would be with English-speaking people on a tour that took me everywhere. Yeah? So why, then, did I feel so alone and wish I knew how to get somewhere?

Grumbling about my poor navigation skills, I decided to go back to the hotel, but when I returned to the previous corner, I couldn't remember which way I'd come.

My footsteps echoed on the cobblestones and I looked in vain for a street sign on a pole. I finally realized the names of the streets were fastened to the stone sides of the buildings. However, with the darkness settling even faster, I could barely see them at all, much less find them useful.

A motorcycle, driven at high speed, zoomed past

me, but no cars. Since I had apparently stumbled into an area of offices, which were now closed for the night, only a few pedestrians hurried by, and they were too far away to speak to. They looked as if they knew where *they* were going, yet never glanced in my direction. Even if they had, I couldn't tell them my problem, my knowledge of Italian being limited to *"Ciao."*

Fear trickled down my spine. I was lost. A woman, all alone in a strange city, and I didn't even know the language. What on earth had made me venture out alone at night? My sometimes poor decision making, that's what. I'd read about pickpockets in large European cities, how women had their purses grabbed from their arms, jewelry snatched from around their necks. I could be mugged, or worse.

I wanted to go back to the hotel, but how? At the corner on which I stood, five exceedingly narrow streets, looking exactly alike, converged. All looked dark and dangerous. Black shadows lengthened on the sides of the buildings. Blown by a breeze, leaves from the pavement swirled around my feet. Blood pounded in my ears. My heart banged in my chest like a metronome gone berserk.

Wanting to run, I found myself rooted to the spot, my legs feeling like iron posts, my arms prickling with cold chills.

I took a deep breath, then another. I scolded myself. Why was I allowing fear to control me? I was a grown woman who lived in what I supposed European citizens would consider a dangerous city. Think of all those murder mysteries set in Los Angeles. Yet, I walked those streets without fear. Well, at least in neighborhoods I knew something about. I closed my eyes and tried to visualize a well-known street in La Brea.

Then I put my new-found confidence to the test. I remembered the first street I had turned into when I left the hotel. I had turned left after one block, then two blocks straight ahead, and then I turned right into the street with the shops closing for the night.

Or was it left? Then...what came next? Which of the streets in front of me had been the one? How did I get to the government offices? Suddenly, my breathing stopped and icicles of fear returned. I heard someone walking behind me, coming closer and closer.

I opened my eyes and turned my head but saw nothing. The person stayed in the shadows, and I imagined him hiding, waiting, ready to pounce. I shivered.

I'd been resourceful in the past, found ways to get out of predicaments—like climbing out on balconies—but this time, no fanciful ideas came to me.

The footsteps came up behind me.

Chapter 4

"Hi, there. Want some company?"

I recognized the voice of Taylor Mitchell, swung around and smiled at him. Okay, I hadn't somehow remembered directions to the hotel. Instead, Taylor had come to my rescue. Unlike the fellow in the old joke who had declined the rowboat, the motorboat and the helicopter, I wasn't about to quibble.

Glad I hadn't met up with a mugger, I had a sudden impulse to want to throw my arms around Taylor. I told myself that would be in gratitude, but I realized the sensation that was stirring in my middle also meant a growing attraction to the guy. All those thoughts of avoiding him dissolved. Maybe we were fated to meet. Maybe we were meant to be together.

"Company would be nice." Then honesty made me admit the truth. "As a matter of fact, I think I'm lost."

He grinned. "I worried that might happen, so I followed you. I hope you don't mind."

"Mind? You saved my life. I have no idea where I am."

"For a while there, I thought you were heading for the Trevi Fountain on your own. You're very close to it, you know."

"Really? I think the Trevi Fountain is on our tour itinerary. However," I added, so he wouldn't think I was brushing him off, "I'd be happy to go there now if you lead the way." Being scared had somehow dampened my hunger pangs.

"Good. We have just time enough to do that before dinner at that restaurant I mentioned."

I quickly agreed. Not only did I need his savvy, but I'd have his company again for dinner. "Provided we go Dutch treat. That's my only condition."

Taylor pretended to frown and then smiled. "Accepted." He took my hand in his and led me down the street.

After a short walk through more narrow streets with no cars, just pedestrians and the ever-popular motorbikes, we sauntered across ancient cobblestones and turned a corner. I saw crowds strolling toward a large structure adorned with many sculptures. When we came nearer, I saw a pool of water glistening with the shine of many coins.

"Here it is, the famous Trevi Fountain. I hope it's what you expected."

I studied it for a moment. "Not exactly. I didn't realize it backed up to a building. I pictured it as a circle with people able to walk all the way around it."

"That's not just any building you see behind it. It's a palace, Palazzo Poli."

"It *is* beautiful." I opened my purse and found a coin. I maneuvered my way between other tourists and down the three shallow steps until I stood closer to the water.

Taylor followed me. "Don't forget to make a wish."

"Isn't that automatic? If you throw a coin in the fountain it means you'll come back to Rome some day, doesn't it?"

"True, but you can make another wish if you like."

My wishes, for the past ten months, had been that I'd get a job and, more recently, that Hardcastle wouldn't fire me from my current one. But I didn't believe in magic fountains, so I just hoped I'd write an article about it Hardcastle would approve.

When I turned again, Taylor's hand reached out to mine, and he guided me back up the steps to the street. "We still have some time before dinner. The restaurant I mentioned isn't too far from here, so we could walk, if that's okay."

"That's fine." In truth, even with the heavier-than-usual shoes I wore, I could feel the cobblestones underfoot. Fortunately, we soon met up with almost-smooth concrete sidewalks, and walking became much easier.

When we turned into yet another street, I paused for a moment. "How do you find your way around? I'm still totally lost. There must be a zillion of these narrow streets, and they all look alike."

"I have a GPS in my brain. Plus, I've been here before, you know."

"I'd have to live here for twenty years before I'd be able to find my way home."

"No, you wouldn't. Small children do it all the time."

"Small children know Italian, too, but I don't."

"Maybe I'll teach you."

"I thought you were just learning, too. Wasn't that a language dictionary you showed me on the plane?"

"Yes, I always brush up a little before I come. Not

that I'm at all fluent." He gestured with his hand. "But I could teach you a few important phrases."

I let that statement pass without comment in case the phrases he meant were X-rated. Besides, we had reached a restaurant with tables set up behind barriers of tubbed plants in the street. "Is this the one?"

"Nope. Just a bit farther."

"No wonder the streets are crowded with cars. The restaurants take some of the parking space at the curbs for their outdoor tables."

"But Italians love to eat out of doors."

"Is that where the term *al fresco* came from?"

"I guess so."

"And there are so many cars. They're parked nose to tail, even in the crosswalks."

"In some places they even park on sidewalks. At least they're small cars and motorbikes. No SUVs."

"I'm not surprised there aren't any SUVs. With the price of gas in Europe, who could afford them? I doubt they get eleven feet to a gallon."

He nodded. "And most of the people who drive them don't carry any cargo heavier than take-out food."

I laughed. "Even with no large vehicles, I think the authorities should put a sign up outside of Rome: 'No more cars may enter until one leaves.'"

"Good thinking." He held my elbow and guided me across the street. "Here's the restaurant I promised."

Unlike so many others I'd seen, its large dining area resided in a piazza, not a narrow street. "Are we going to dine *al fresco*?"

"No, we're going inside. I want you to hear the opera singers."

"They have opera singers?"

"Italy is famous for its music, you know, especially opera."

Of course I knew. I wasn't that culturally impoverished. "I've heard of La Scala," I added in my own defense.

"I don't think these singers are with La Scala, but they sound pretty good to me. And they don't just sing operatic arias. I expect you'll recognize some lighter songs, even a Broadway show-tune or two."

Inside the dimly lit restaurant, I could make out frescoes on the walls, low wrought-iron fences that separated one floor level from another, just a foot or so higher, and charming glass and metal lamps on white cloth-covered tables. I followed a waiter in black trousers, white shirt and bow tie to a table for two in a corner.

"Is this all right?" Taylor asked. "We'll be able to see and hear the singers but not be so close we can't carry on a conversation."

"It's fine." I folded my sweater over the back of the chair and sat down. Then the waiter pulled my napkin from the water glass and draped it across my lap before handing me a menu as large as a billboard.

When the waiter left, I grinned. "I do love being pampered."

Taylor glanced approvingly at me. "And anyone as pretty as you are deserves to be."

Embarrassed by the compliment, I hid behind the menu. Although written in Italian, English explanations were printed below the dinner selections, and I had no problem agreeing with Taylor's choices of minestrone soup, penne pasta and chicken piccata.

Taylor glanced around. "We're early. This place is quite popular and will be filled in another hour or so."

"They won't chase us out before the singers arrive, will they?"

"Nope." He smiled at me again.

I grew nervous and scrounged for something to say to break the silence. "Thanks again for rescuing me tonight. Anyone as directionally impaired as I am ought not to be allowed out without a keeper."

"But you travel all over Los Angeles for your job, don't you? How do you manage?"

"Very poorly. I start out two hours early, so I have time to ask directions at every gas station I pass." I hadn't exaggerated by much.

He laughed. "Maybe you should get a GPS for your car."

"I plan to, but at the moment I can't afford the kind of cars that have them. I'm still paying off student loans."

"Did you study journalism in college?"

"Yes. What about you? Did you study art?"

"No, I studied engineering."

"Really? Was your father an engineer? Did he want you to follow in his footsteps?"

Our soup arrived, and, by the time the waiter finished placing the bowls before us and offering a basket of bread, Taylor either forgotten or ignored my question. "Computers are my hobby."

"You said it pays for your lifestyle. How does that work?"

"I live in Arizona, and, as I'm sure you know, a lot

of older people retire there. Senior citizen complexes are one of the fastest-growing businesses in the southwest."

"And—" I prompted, taking a piece of bread from the basket.

"And these communities have computer labs where people learn how to use them to keep in touch with their children by e-mail. They like to get current pictures of their grandchildren, and some even write their memoirs."

"So do you teach those classes?"

"Yes, it works out perfectly because they're always held in the winter months. In summer, when it's too hot in Phoenix, the snowbirds flock back to the cooler climate they came from."

"I'd think that working only part-time wouldn't be very lucrative. Is the salary you get for teaching that good?"

"Not as good as I'd like, but some of those people are quite wealthy, so I also give private instructions and do trouble-shooting. Plus I moonlight sometimes as a consultant for businesses in the area."

"That must pay well since it lets you take so much time off. You can obviously afford to do some traveling as well."

"I have a confession to make. I'm independently, er, comfortable. I started a small software business while in college, and a couple of years ago I sold it for a nice hunk of change."

"Good for you."

"The company gave me more money than I'd ever seen at one time, so I handed it over to a financial advisor and he gives me some of the interest it earns whenever I run low on cash."

He turned his attention to the food and seemed to consider the subject of his career closed. While I pondered that and wondered what other topic we could discuss, we finished the soup.

I remembered the tour. "So you got a place on the tour after all."

"Yes, one couple dropped out, it seems, leaving only eight of us. I talked to Enza on the phone and she said we'll be three couples, plus a single woman and her young daughter."

I looked over at him. "You mean us? We're not a couple."

"I didn't mean to imply a relationship. I just meant that I'm a man and you're a woman, and I guess that makes us a couple."

I didn't respond to that and changed the subject. "Have you been to this restaurant before?" The question sounded lame, even to me.

"Yes, but I came alone the other times."

"I recall you said on the plane that you were a loner, but here you are with me. I think you've been exceptionally outgoing, for a loner."

"Well, I'm trying not to be like that anymore." The waiter removed our soup bowls and Taylor continued. "You were so friendly on the plane, and, like I said, I'm trying to be more open with people. I sort of made it my goal to accomplish a break-through on this trip."

"You're doing a good job."

"Can I quote you on that?"

"Why? Do you need a recommendation?"

"Only to a counselor near my home."

My face warmed, and I wondered why he'd mentioned something I considered somewhat personal. "And has going to the counselor helped?"

"Without boring you with the details, I'll just say we're making progress." He paused, and a frown crossed his forehead. "I'm sorry. I know people aren't supposed to discuss personal matters on first dates, but—"

"That's okay," I assured him. "In the first place, I don't consider this a date. We're just having dinner together because otherwise I'd get lost again."

The waiter brought our pasta, and I waited until he left. "I would imagine lots of people see, er, counselors these days. I don't mind your talking about it. Life is pretty stressful, so, whatever works."

We ate in silence for a few minutes. My thoughts flew in sequence to what he'd just told me, and I decided to share my own experiences with him.

"Everyone has issues of some kind. Sometimes it helps to talk to someone."

"Who do you talk to?"

"Well, I have wonderful parents, and now we live close enough to visit often. My sister lives in Texas, not California, but we keep in touch regularly. She's older than I am, and married with two children."

He didn't say anything, and I felt awkward, rattling on, but I couldn't seem to stop. "Plus I have an older brother." Again, he didn't comment. "And I had wonderful friends in college and now a good job that I like."

This condensed story of my life apparently didn't

mean anything to him, and I felt foolish for having said so much. Like I'd once again put my mouth in gear before engaging my brain. Didn't Miss Manners say the secret to being a good conversationalist is letting the other person talk? So I said, "Tell me about your family. Do they live in Arizona, too?"

Just then the waiter removed our plates and brought the next course, and the music began, provided by six formally-dressed men, effectively making conversation difficult, if not impossible. I listened in silence, wondering why Taylor had opened the subject of his counselor and then dropped it so suddenly.

Three singers—two men in tuxedos and an attractive blonde woman wearing a long flowered dress—appeared next and performed in a twenty-minute set, and, as Taylor had predicted, they were very good. Besides some opera arias I recognized, I enjoyed their versions of songs from *The Sound of Music, The King and I,* and *My Fair Lady.* They sang one chorus of each first in English and then in Italian.

As soon as the performers took their bows, the waiter presented the bill. Taylor tried to pay the entire amount, but I reminded him of our agreement and put my share on the tray.

He shrugged and then brightened. "The best gelato in Rome isn't too far from here."

I was grateful for the return of his bright mood. "Lead me to it. I adore gelato."

"Then you've had it before?"

"It's Italian ice cream, isn't it? Los Angeles can provide almost anything if you know where to look for it."

"Good." He got up and pulled my chair back. "Then we can walk back to the hotel to burn off the calories."

Outside, Taylor put my sweater over my shoulders, and we passed little shops that occupied the first floors of what seemed to be more apartment buildings. After turning several corners, we finally came to the gelato shop. I ordered chocolate.

"The perfect choice." Taylor ordered the same.

"I want to pay for mine."

However, this time he wouldn't budge. He pulled out some euros and paid for both. "You're being rather picky about this Dutch treat business."

I didn't answer, accepted my cone from the server, and left the shop. As we walked, we talked again about movies and discovered we liked the same kinds of films. In addition, we were both avid readers, and I found he read not only fiction best sellers, but also non-fiction books on serious subjects, like politics, the cosmos and religion. While listening to his opinions, I almost forgot my surroundings until I found myself back at the hotel again.

"Thanks for the gelato. It's probably just as well I don't know my way around Rome. If I did, I'd go there for gelato every day and gain at least ten pounds before I left town."

"Even if you did, you'd lose it again with all the walking we'll be doing."

I glanced up at him. "How do you know we'll do a lot of walking? I thought we go places in a van."

"That's just between cities, according to Enza. In town, we'll walk a lot, and, since I read the itinerary and I've been here before, I know the distances between the various sights."

He insisted on going up in the elevator with me and seeing me to my door before he went to his own room. He took the key from my hand, inserted it in the lock, and returned it. Then, when he placed the key in my open palm, he held onto my hand for a long moment.

The warm pressure felt comfortable, but finally I pulled free, at the same time hoping not to seem rude.

He frowned. "Sorry. I guess I'm trying too hard again."

"Trying how?"

"To be more... you know..."

My earlier curiosity returned. "Did you have no brothers or sisters? Is that why you said you're a loner?"

"I'm sorry. I shouldn't have said so much." He cleared his throat and backed away. "Good night."

I entered my room and closed the door. What was that all about? I wouldn't have minded a little flirtation as part of my itinerary. He had come to my rescue on the street and had a great personality. Most women would jump at the chance to become at least a little involved, but he seemed ambivalent.

I didn't want him to pretend we were a "couple," at least not yet, but Taylor's behavior puzzled me. One moment he spoke openly, like an old friend, and the next, he seemed secretive and silent. I remembered that, on at least two occasions in the restaurant, he failed to answer questions about his family. Why? My weird imagination took off. Were they midgets? In the witness-protection program? CIA spies?

Why did he seem to regret having called himself a loner, and why did he not want to talk about his past? Why frown and back away like that? What was he hiding?

Chapter 5

Day Three

Still thinking about Taylor, I didn't fall asleep right away that night, and I woke up the next day with him on my mind again. During our pleasant evening, I'd had feelings of elation that I'd finally met a man who was gentlemanly and polite as well as intelligent and well-read. Like he'd time-traveled from an earlier century. Most guys I met were about as deep as a Pet Rock. The heaviest thinking they did involved sports teams, and they thought weekends were for watching ten consecutive hours of football on televison.

If conversations ever got around to serious subjects they'd say things like, "Oh, yeah, I know what's going on in the world," or, "I used to read the newspapers, but..." or "I've seen an opera." Probably not since they were dragged there by their schoolteachers. Sometimes they'd go so far as to say they believe it's important for families to have strong moral values. It always sounded suspiciously like a ploy to make me think that—although they might seem superficial right then—they were trainable.

But Taylor was already there, and I felt as if the French family who needed to sit together had been responsible for dropping him in that airplane seat next to me. Still, later he'd acted so strange when I asked about his family. My wild imagination took off again, and I wondered if he killed them all and confessed his crime to that counselor. Weren't priests and counselors supposed to keep confidences like that, even from the police?

Then I told myself I'd been watching too many courtroom dramas on television and climbed out of bed.

After showering and dressing, I went down to the restaurant, which I found open and bustling with customers. My itinerary said there would be a continental breakfast, and I approached the tables lined up along the walls. I nearly gasped at the array of food: cereal, bread, rolls and croissants, and bowls of mixed fresh fruit. Covered containers kept scrambled eggs, bacon and sausages hot, and large plates displayed cold meats and cheeses. Pitchers of fruit juice and milk rested near urns of coffee and hot water. What a feast! In U.S. hotels, a continental breakfast sometimes meant only orange juice, coffee and a sweet roll.

Not one to pass up free food, even if my body didn't need it, I filled a small bowl with fruit and a plate with eggs, a slice of ham, and a croissant. I used the carafe of hot water to make a cup of tea and then found a small vacant table in a corner. Having already noted the sunny and warm weather outside, I hoped to sit near a window, but the restaurant's only windows faced an atrium surrounded by the hotel lobby on three sides and a blank wall on the fourth. Yet, the room seemed bright and cheerful, with paintings of Italian scenes on the cream-colored walls and fuchsia napkins at every place.

Being a naturally curious person, and, trust me, this helps if you're going to be a reporter, I glanced around at the other people in the dining room while I ate. I saw mostly couples of varying ages, plus two middle-aged women seated together, a family of four, and several gentlemen sitting alone reading newspapers.

A young man, dressed like a member of an ugly-clothing required society, came in and headed immediately for the coffee, as if it were an antidote to poison someone forced him to drink. Even from where I sat, I could tell his blood content was eighty percent Jim Beam. Fortunately, after drinking two cups of black coffee in rapid succession, he left the dining room, taking his body odor with him.

It occurred to me that some of the other people in the dining room might be on my tour, which would start in a few hours, but I had no way of knowing. Then I remembered that the tour guide, Enza, would be picking up some of them at the airport that morning, so they had probably not arrived yet.

Since I'd enjoyed my simple breakfast, I debated returning to the buffet table and heaping my plate all over again, but I decided being able to zip my pants was probably more important, since my one suitcase contained all the clothes I'd brought. Yet I did go back to pour more grapefruit juice, at which time I noticed an attractive, thirty-something woman and a teen-aged girl discussing the bounty laid out before them. They were American, judging by the woman's somewhat loud voice, and—whereas sometimes I eavesdrop on other people's conversation deliberately—this time I had no choice but to hear it. The woman had a lot to say about the girl's selections.

"No eggs or sausage," she told her. "Just cereal and some fruit." She put a banana on her daughter's plate. "And a hard roll, but only one pat of butter."

"Oh, Mom," the girl muttered.

The mother was slender, with short, perfectly-coiffed blonde hair, and the daughter, also slender, but slightly shorter than her mother, had long, straight blonde hair fastened behind her ears with twin blue barrettes. She flushed under her mother's instructions but didn't protest. I admired her attitude. To nobody's surprise, teenagers rejected everything their parents told them and went out of their way to rebel. I mean, like, didn't I do it myself at that age? Nowadays, however, the teen years seemed to start at nine.

However, this girl took instruction calmly. The pair took a table not far from my own, and I found myself watching them over the rim of my glass. The mother's voice carried all over the room, and, finally having heard more than I cared to, I wished I had something to read. However, I couldn't read the Italian newspapers and hadn't brought my guidebook down with me.

Still trapped into overhearing, I realized the mother gave many orders to her daughter, who kept her head down as she ate her breakfast and, if she replied at all, did so in a voice so low I didn't hear it. Her back to me, she occasionally shifted uneasily in her chair, and once looked around before returning her gaze to her plate. She wore blue slacks, not jeans, a pink short-sleeved blouse and a multi-colored vest. On the other hand, her mother seemed overdressed in a gray knee-length skirt, made of a soft jersey fabric, and a matching, long-sleeved tunic top with a cowl neckline that dipped rather low in front, revealing more cleavage than seemed appropriate for eight in the morning.

Something about the woman, aside from her loud voice and constant frown while speaking to her daughter, bothered me. I turned aside and looked at the plants in the atrium, reminding myself not to be judgmental.

"Good morning."

I turned from the window to see Taylor, filled plate in one hand and coffee cup in the other, standing next to my table. "May I join you?"

"Of course." I smiled, glad to take my mind off the other couple.

"Get a good night's sleep?" He placed his food on the table and sat down opposite me.

"Yes. How about you?"

"Like the proverbial top." He dropped the napkin into his lap. "You look very nice."

"Thank you." I tried not to let his compliment affect me. Unlike the woman I'd been watching for the past ten minutes, I wore a simple outfit: navy slacks, white blouse, and my go-everywhere cardigan sweater in case I needed it. I didn't know about Italy, but in Los Angeles many places were air conditioned to a level cold enough to kill small birds.

My thoughts returned to the night before, when Taylor had behaved so strangely, but that morning he was jolly again, so I decided to enjoy his good mood rather than press him about the previous one.

"Thanks again for rescuing me last night. I enjoyed

the dinner and the singers. As well as the gelato."

"I'm glad you liked them." He sipped his coffee. "I meant to ask you yesterday how it happens that you're writing about this tour, but have no camera. Won't you need pictures to go along with your article?"

"Actually I have a small camera for my own use, not to illustrate my article. The magazine doesn't need the pictures I might take, even if I had a fancy camera like yours."

"Is a photographer joining you then?"

"No, the tour company owners have already provided marvelous photographs they want us to use. They sent some to the office and said if I need more to just ask."

"I see." He dug into his sausages, eggs, fruit and cheese and changed the subject again. "I love continental breakfasts, don't you?"

I repeated aloud what I'd been thinking earlier. "This is a far cry from what they call a continental breakfast in some hotels back home."

"I guess Europeans like a hearty meal, but not all hotels in Italy offer this much."

Since they were in my line of sight, I noticed the woman and her daughter get up to leave, the mother pushing the girl ahead. I had finished as well, so I reached down and picked up my purse.

Taylor rose. "Oh, don't go. Have another cup of coffee and keep me company." He reached for my cup. "Black? Sugar? Cream?"

"No coffee." I shook my head. "Thanks anyway." I remembered how much I hated eating alone and thought he might feel the same. "But I will stay if you like."

He sat down again. "We have a couple of hours to kill before we meet Enza for the tour. What shall we do?"

There he went again, assuming we should spend all our time together. I enjoyed his company and was tempted, but what about his occasional evasiveness?

I hedged, saying the first thing that came into my mind. "I thought I might go back up to my room for awhile, and do the reading I was supposed to do."

"On a fine day like this? Besides, you'll learn more by seeing the actual sights. Don't you want to explore the city?"

I grinned. "And get lost again?"

"I'll go with you and make sure you're okay."

He was right, and I knew I shouldn't coop myself up in the hotel room. Besides, how often would I get to Rome? The tour probably couldn't cover everything to see in the city in only three days. But should I go exploring with him?

"I don't want to monopolize your time. Maybe you have things to do. You said on the plane that you expected to spend some time in Rome before going to Lake Como."

"I just planned to wander around the city, but it's much more fun to do it with someone else."

"My, you stopped being a loner in a hurry. Or was that just a line to arouse my sympathy?"

"Praise the Lord, I'm cured!" Then he laughed at himself. "Seriously, I enjoyed showing you the Trevi Fountain last night." He paused again. "I know this sounds like a line or at the very least a cliché, but I'd—

well, I'd like to get to know you better. I *was* a loner. I don't know why you should show up in my life and make me different, but there it is." He shrugged.

His words reminded me of my own thoughts, but I felt the need to be truthful. "I don't think I'm the one who made you want to be different. You said your counselor is helping you."

"Well, then, maybe you're the answer to his prayers."

I couldn't help smiling. "I guess I can't quarrel with that." I rose from my seat.

He pushed his chair back and got up. "Let's start, shall we?"

The word "start" made me think of the start of something between us after all. In spite of an occasional niggling doubt, I decided I liked that.

Chapter 6

I looked at my watch. "Actually we don't have much time. We're supposed to meet the tour group in the lobby at eleven, and I don't want to be late."

"We won't be." He guided me through the lobby and out onto the street, and, the weather being quite warm, I tied the sleeves of my sweater around my waist. We walked four blocks—past shops that, except for signs in Italian, looked very much like those in any American city—to a square with a church at one end and a gurgling fountain in the center.

"Are we going inside the church?"

"Not unless you really want to, although it's much grander on the inside than it is on the outside." He waved toward the building. "On the other hand, you'll see lots of grand churches on the tour anyway."

"I'll leave it up to you. If you've been here before, perhaps you don't want to bother going through it again."

He thought for a moment. "How would you like to see the manger where Jesus lay?"

I stared silently for a moment. "Yeah. Right."

Taylor shrugged.

I let a beat go by. "Are you serious? The real manger is here? In this church?"

"That's what they claim. It's behind glass, covered in silver and doesn't look like any manger I ever saw, but then what do I know?"

I'm usually a bit gullible, but that time I felt a load of skepticism. Besides, there was something about the way Taylor described it that made me hesitate.

"Well—"

He didn't answer, just took my hand and led me inside the church. It was heavily decorated with paintings and statues everywhere. Arches containing small altars stood before stained glass windows. We passed confessionals that resembled tall dark wooden boxes lining one wall, with signs overhead indicating which language one could confess in. Or, I corrected myself, perhaps that meant the language the priest understood.

Before I could study all the sights that met my gaze, Taylor led me to the front of the main altar and down a staircase that curved toward a sunken shrine. About four feet wide and three feet high, the glass-fronted box, just as he'd described it, held a silver-covered object. It stood on a pedestal and was so decorated with filigree and curlicues, that I found it hard to believe it might have been a small manger at one time. The mangers I'd seen in those little Christmas tableaus were made of sticks or slats of wood and always had straw in them. Had they silvered that as well, or was I being picky?

I spoke my thoughts out loud. "It looks like an ornate soup tureen."

Taylor squelched a guffaw and grabbed my hand. "Why don't we just look at the outside?" He almost dragged me back up the stairs and out of doors into the warm sunshine. I had embarrassed myself again.

"I'm sorry—"

He laughed out loud. "Don't give it another thought."

"I didn't mean to—"

"It's okay. Actually, I think you described it perfectly." We both laughed so hard that I think he wiped tears from his eyes.

After a minute I cleared my throat. "You're not Catholic, and you told me you've done your traveling alone, with no tour guide, so how come you know so much about the church?"

"I read about it, of course. Books are a great resource, you know." He said it with a grin, not condescendingly, so I grinned back, but I felt the need to defend myself anyway.

"I do have a guidebook, and, if I'd known more than three days beforehand that I was coming here, I'd have certainly read up on it."

"I wasn't being critical. In fact, I enjoy sharing what little information I've picked up."

As I walked across the plaza, I wished I had brought my notebook along in case he wanted to add more information.

He didn't. "We could feed the pigeons."

I laughed at his abrupt change of subject, and he approached a small, wizened old man in a too-large black coat and bought a bag of seeds. We threw the seeds onto the ground, and a flock of pigeons appeared immediately and surrounded us, making short work of the goodies.

When the seeds were gone, we sat on a stone bench and watched an old woman come up to the fountain and fill two plastic jars with water from a spigot.

"Is the water safe to drink?" I asked Taylor.

"Oh, yes, all the water in Italy is okay."

The woman hobbled off with her jars, and a middle-aged man who had been sitting on another bench nearby also got up and walked away. He left a newspaper behind, so Taylor retrieved it and read the headline out loud.

"Election to be held Sunday."

I remembered seeing colorful signs that looked like election posters at every corner we passed on the way to the church. "You can translate that? I thought you were just beginning to learn Italian."

"I pick up a little more every time I come. Anyway, my translation may not be exactly right, but it's close enough."

"What else does it say?"

He cleared his throat, and, in sonorous tones, pretended to read. "Signore Giuseppe Stallone, a distant cousin of the American actor Sylvester Stallone, is running for dog-catcher of Rome."

"You're joking."

Taylor ignored me and kept on with his own version of an article. "Signore Stallone says he is admirably suited to this position as he has been an animal-hater for many years. His niece, Alissa, the famous fashion model, often wears a bikini swimsuit made of dog fur."

I slapped him playfully on the arm. "Stop."

Taylor put down the paper. "Well, if you don't want to know what's going on in the world, don't blame me." He looked at his watch. "I guess it's time to go back to the hotel anyway."

Still grinning, I fell in step beside him. I could be very happy, I realized, spending a lot of time at his side. What a lucky break that Taylor had taken the seat next to me on the flight and would now be on my tour.

Ten minutes later, after we took a shortcut through a section of what appeared to be a commuter train station, we arrived at the hotel and entered the lobby, which overflowed with people.

I noticed a tall, handsome woman in her early forties, with thick, black hair pulled back from her face, a Roman nose, and sparkling brown eyes, who seemed to be scanning everyone who came through the doors. She wore a tailored suit and stout shoes, which, to my eyes, didn't strike me as tourist clothes. I looked questioningly at Taylor while nodding in her direction.

"I think you're right. That must be Enza." He pulled me along, stopped in front of the woman and introduced us. "I'm Taylor Mitchell, and this is Sydney Cooke. Are you Enza, our tour guide?"

"Welcome. Yes, I am Enza, and we are all here now." Her voice, clear and pleasant, carried only a faint Italian accent. "I will introduce you to the others." She repeated our names, and then waved an arm toward a gray-haired couple who appeared to be in their sixties or seventies. "Signore John and Signora Mary Parker. They come from the Louisiana."

Taylor and I moved forward and shook hands with the older man and his wife.

"And," Enza went on, "may I present Signora Robin and Signore Lance Waxman. They are from Chicago, and they are on their honeymoon."

By the way Lance's arm circled his bride's waist, I could have guessed they were newlyweds. Everyone in the little group applauded, and then Taylor and I shook hands with them.

Enza moved finally to the single woman and her daughter. "Signora Karen Vale and Signorina Kimberly."

I did a double-take. Karen Vale was the woman I had seen in the restaurant that morning and Kimberly was the daughter. I hadn't known they'd be on my tour.

"Do call me Karen," the woman said. She moved straight to Taylor, took his hand and smiled up at him. "I'm so glad to meet you." She pushed her daughter forward, as if the introduction was a necessary, but unpleasant, ritual. "This is Kim, thirteen going on thirty." She laughed as she said it, but I could tell Kimberly didn't care for her mother's comment.

I stood quietly, thoughts swirling in my brain—unkind thoughts I must admit—until I realized that Karen Vale had never acknowledged me and continued to clutch Taylor's hand. Then, instead of retreating, the unkind thoughts grew and expanded like science fiction movie fungus.

Can you blame me? Just when I thought I'd met a great guy, along came competition.

Chapter 7

I told myself not to think like that. Anyway, why should I get upset because Karen Vale was clinging like Crazy Glue to Taylor, or that she and her daughter were on my tour? Six other people would be there too. Perhaps I'd judged the woman too hastily. Just because she seemed a bit bossy toward her daughter didn't mean she'd be an unpleasant companion on the tour. As for her apparent impulsive interest in Taylor, I had no right to be concerned about that, either. Taylor was not my boyfriend.

Of course not. So why was my stomach feeling like I'd swallowed a live frog? I had a sudden realization that, in just two days, I'd begun to consider Taylor more than a mere acquaintance. Plus, everyone over the age of twenty-one knows that when romance rears it head, logic flies out the window.

Before I could think more about it, Enza announced we would begin immediately and herded us all from the hotel and into a white van parked at the curb. Since I'd been standing closest to the door and approached the van before the others, I boarded first and took a seat on the left side, directly behind the driver. He was a forty-something dark-haired man with a thick mustache, wearing rimmed glasses and a bright yellow sweater.

Although the van held seats for at least twelve

people, the couples sat together, and Taylor claimed the seat next to me, which did a lot to calm down my imaginary frog. Enza sat alone across the aisle, close enough to the driver so she could inform him, in rapid Italian, where she wanted him to go.

She also spoke to the rest of us, explaining that we would go to the Piazza Navona and the Trevi Fountain before stopping for lunch. She described what we were about to see, leaving no time for conversation of our own. That was fine with me. I hadn't a clue what to say to Taylor. My mind seemed concentrated on the way Karen Vale had held his hand. I longed to know what he thought about her, but I didn't want to bring up that particular subject.

When the van stopped and we got off in a narrow street, Enza waved us on, walking as she talked, saying that our van, like all other vehicles, was not allowed in the piazza.

No vehicles, true, but the enormous plaza was ringed with beautiful buildings five and six stories high. Tourists like us crowded the area. Vendors sold paintings or colorful scarves and postcards, and tables were set up in front of restaurants. Fountains and statues dotted the center of the plaza.

Taylor had wandered off, but I stayed close to Enza so I could learn as much as possible for my magazine article. She pointed to the tall obelisk and said the ancient Romans had brought it back from Egypt at the time of Cleopatra.

Enza suggested we take our time wandering around the piazza and she would wait for us at the south entrance, so I took the opportunity to observe the artwork for sale by, presumably, the artists themselves. I hoped to find a souvenir to take back with me, but none of the paintings captured the exact scene I wanted. Probably just as well, since my only suitcase was already quite full and I didn't want to go through the hassle of shipping something home, assuming I could even afford it.

Mary Parker, who wore a Pashmina shawl that matched her gray hair around her shoulders, strolled up to my side and seemed to be doing the same thing. "We collect paintings from all our trips." She smiled as if visualizing a magnificent collection. "I have a pen and ink drawing from London and a watercolor from Paris. And, of course, many oil paintings."

"Is this your first trip to Italy?"

"Yes. Maybe our last trip to Europe. We're getting too old to keep up with all you young people."

I scoffed at the idea. "No, you're not. You don't seem to have any trouble walking. As long as you can do that, you're fine."

"That's one reason I chose this tour over some others. It leaves most afternoons free, and I can rest in the hotel room."

"Not this afternoon, though."

"No, but there's so much to see in Rome." She looked around. "Where's your young man?"

"I beg your pardon?" I asked the question, even though I was fairly certain she meant Taylor. "Oh, you mean Mr. Mitchell."

"Yes. You're traveling together, aren't you?"

"No, not really." I hesitated, not wanting to go into the long story of my meeting with Taylor. "We met because we both happened to get to Rome a day early."

"I see." She frowned. "I didn't mean to offend you. Young people nowadays— well, you know what I mean. They don't seem to find it necessary to be married, but they act like married people, even travel together."

"Yes, I guess some do." I knew several couples who lived together without benefit of marriage, but I didn't want to do that. Even if my parents wouldn't go ballistic, which they would, my practical nature would prevent my following this seemingly ever-growing phenomenon.

My own mother grew up during the so-called "sexual revolution" of the '60s and '70s, but she seemed immune to it. She got married, and—although she and I often disagreed on other things—I planned to do the same. I mean, what's the point of striving for equal pay for equal work—and, forty years later, there's still a lot to be done in *that* department—and having control of our own destiny, if we're going to just live with a man and then have nothing to show for it in the end? Not that financial security was my main reason, but, laws being what they were, you had to be married to inherit the property you both worked for.

Mrs. Parker looked away, as if embarrassed to have talked about unmarried couples when, for all she knew, I might have a live-in lover of my own back home.

She turned back to me for a moment, "Well, I think I'll join Enza now." She smiled and moved off.

In spite of my thoughts, as I walked to the south end of the piazza, I found myself looking for Taylor. I spotted him flanked by Karen Vale on one side and

Kimberly on the other. His height, between the two
short women, made the trio look like a sandwich cookie
with the filling coming out. I smiled at the thought,
although I wondered unhappily if the three of them
linking arms that way would get to be a habit.

When they, along with the Waxmans and Parkers,
reached Enza, we all headed off down a narrow street
leading away from the plaza. We soon found ourselves
at the Trevi Fountain. I enjoyed its look by day but
didn't go down the steps that time and throw in a coin
as I'd done the night before.

"We have to stop meeting this way. People will
talk."

Even before I saw him, I recognized Taylor's voice
and turned around. The frog in my middle woke up.
"Oh? What will they say?"

"That I enjoy your company and want to be with
you."

"I doubt they'll say that about us. You and the
Vales, perhaps." As soon as I said the words, I regretted
them. All too often, I speak first and wish later I could
take back what I'd said. Taylor would think I was
jealous, and I wasn't. At least I wasn't supposed to be.
I told myself again that I came there to do a job, not
start a romance.

Taylor didn't seem to notice, or care about, my
comment. "Mrs. Vale is one of those women who feels
incomplete without a man to take care of her, explain
things, and make her feel secure. And I seem to be the
only otherwise unattached male."

"She seems a very, er, charming person." I hoped
the compliment sounded sincere. I'd had unflattering

thoughts about her so far, but I kept telling myself I shouldn't judge people so quickly, if ever. Besides, since we were all on the same tour, we'd have to get along.

"Kimberly is a sweet child," Taylor said. "And I've been here before, so I don't mind sharing what little I know with her. It's the least I can do."

As if summoned by our conversation, Kimberly rushed toward us, her mother inevitably close behind. "I threw a coin in the fountain," the girl said, her voice high with excitement. "That means I'll come back to Rome again some day, doesn't it?"

"So they say." Taylor smiled at her, and she put her hand in his, almost, I thought, as if he were her father.

Karen Vale acknowledged me with a look that was almost a sneer. As if she thought I was in desperate need of a hygiene product. Then she turned her attention back to Taylor. "You must tell us all about this magnificent fountain."

"I think you should ask Enza. She's the expert."

Undeterred, Karen Vale went on. "What is it supposed to represent? How old is it? Did the ancient Romans build it?"

"No, I think it's more like the 18th century."

"So recent?" She sounded disappointed.

"You'll see plenty of other ancient sights everywhere we go in Italy."

Karen asked Taylor about the statue above the water, turning toward it, her back to me and effectively excluding me from their little group. I shrugged and walked back toward the others.

Next we were guided to the Pantheon, and I listened both to Enza's explanations and Taylor's answering Karen and Kimberly's myriad questions.

"I was an engineer," John Parker told us, "and learned about this remarkable building when I was a student in college. It's one of the reasons I always wanted to come here."

The thirty-foot hole in the top of the dome, Enza explained, was designed to allow smoke to escape. She told us that animals were regularly sacrificed as burnt offerings to the many gods the people once worshipped.

Kimberly sounded shocked. "They killed animals in here? How gross."

"Now, of course," Enza said, "they do not kill animals, and it is a Christian church."

She took us to lunch at an outdoor café in the plaza in front of the Pantheon, and our entire group clustered around two round tables to eat pizza and fruit. I found myself sitting next to Kimberly at one table, while her mother sat next to Taylor at the other.

I decided to strike up a conversation with the girl. I had no knowledge of Italy to share, but the tour included no one else her age, and I wanted to make her feel welcome.

"I love pizza, don't you?"

"Oh, yes." Kimberly grinned before taking a rather large bite of hers. "Of course, this is different from what we get at home. They don't put as much different stuff on it."

"I suppose you could say we've Americanized it. I like it plain like this myself."

"Oh, I do too." She took a gulp of her Coca-Cola. "I think it's funny though."

"What's funny?"

"My mother doesn't like me to eat fast food, but here people.eat it all the time. While we were riding in the van, I saw dozens of signs for pizza shops." She grinned again and took another bite.

"Your mother probably wants you to eat a balanced diet, including fruits and vegetables." Whether she did or not, it seemed the politically correct thing to say.

"I guess." She paused for another sip of Coke. "I know it's good for me, but, when I'm with my friends, well, you know."

"I'm sure you want to be able to do the same things your friends do."

"Yeah, but it'll get better. I'll be fourteen next month and maybe I'll get to go more places and do more stuff."

I remembered the conversation I'd overheard in the dining room that morning, and I stuck with my decision to give the woman the benefit of the doubt. "Mothers always want what's best for their children."

"It's like, 'Do as I say, not as I do,' isn't it?"

"What do you mean?"

"Well, like after I go to bed at night, she drinks vodka and stuff like that. *That's* not exactly health food."

I paused before answering, not wanting to take sides. "Grown-ups can do things children shouldn't. When you're older—"

"Yeah, I hear that all the time."

I leaned closer. "You'll have lots more years as a grown-up than as a child. How old is your grandfather?"

"Pretty old, I guess, and I have a great-grandmother who's ninety-two." She said it with pride.

"Well, then, if you live that long, you'll have over seventy years to do whatever you like."

"But it'll be seven more years before I'm even twenty-one."

"You may not think so now, but the time will fly by. Besides, you may not want to drink alcohol then. Many grown-ups don't drink at all."

Kimberly stared at me for a moment, as if thinking seriously about the subject. After awhile she spoke again. "I didn't mean to put down my mom. I really love her, and I know it's not easy being a single mother."

"So your father—?"

"They're divorced. Just as well too. She says they did nothing but scream at each other all the time."

"You don't see him? You don't remember him?"

"I remember him. He moved away, got married again and has another family. I get birthday and Christmas presents."

"That's, er, good anyway." I felt my comment to be inadequate, but the girl seemed to have accepted her situation with good grace.

"Everybody's divorced. I have only one friend at school who lives with her real mother and father." She pushed her empty plate aside and drank the last of her Coke before looking up at me. "What about you? Are you married or divorced?"

"Single. Never married and I have no children."

"That's too bad." Like she thought I was over the hill and would never get the chance. After a long moment, she put her hand in mine. "But you're still very pretty. If you want, you can call me Kim."

Oh, good. I had a precocious thirteen-year-old for a friend. But her compliment made me smile anyway. Dare I hope that a certain young man agreed with her opinion?

Chapter 8

When we left the outdoor café, Kim stayed at my side. I wondered if she did so from a desire to offer comfort in my presumably lonely state or to let her mother have some time alone with Taylor.

When we reached the Spanish Steps, I relished the sight of the well-known landmark. Enza told us that artists once flocked there and artist-model wannabes posed on the steps in hopes of getting jobs. However, as a writer myself, I was most intrigued to learn that Keats, Shelley and other English poets visited or lived in the neighborhood.

Soon a downpour of rain pelted us. Vendors, who'd been offering picture postcards only a moment before, suddenly sprouted umbrellas for sale, and I couldn't help admiring their versatility.

With Enza in the lead, our little group scurried down a narrow street, trying to stay under awnings and other overhangs until we reached the spot where the van picked us up for the ride back to the hotel. Laughing and shaking water from our hair and clothes, we boarded the van, and Taylor claimed the seat next to me again. We didn't speak much, however, for the trip back was quite short, and our driver sped even faster than on the way there.

Once in my room, I hustled out of my wet things, showered, and put on dry clothes. Seated at the small desk in the room, I pulled out my notebook and jotted down things I'd seen and heard that I wanted to remember. Later, I lay across the bed to rest, while I listened to the rain drops outside my windows.

The rain stopped falling by early evening, and we were all invited to dine together that night at a restaurant "only fifteen minutes away," according to Enza. "It is not raining, so we will walk, no?"

We walked, yes. I thought I heard a groan go up from Mary Parker, but the older couple followed along behind and arrived less than a minute after the rest of us. Actually, our number grew to twelve, because Enza's husband joined us and so did the owner of the tour company and his wife, who happened to be in Rome on business. They sat at the opposite end of the table from me and, except for introductions, I didn't get to speak to them.

Once more Kim sat next to me and told me about her school and her friends. She also seemed to be trying to emphasize how close she and her mother were, perhaps making up for her negative comments earlier that day. Eventually I tried to turn the conversation to food. The dinner was excellent, but every time Karen refilled her glass from the many bottles of wine on the table, Kim frowned and returned to the subject of her mother's good qualities.

"I think my mother is pretty, don't you?"

"Yes, very."

"Do you think Mr. Mitchell likes her?"

I swallowed hard. Obviously Karen's interest in Taylor hadn't gone unnoticed by her teenaged daughter. I managed to answer in a noncommittal tone.

"I couldn't say."

"I think he does. She needs someone you know, and he seems nice. He's awfully smart too."

I hedged. "It's only the first day, a little early. Perhaps she won't like him when she knows him better."

Why had I said that? Wishful thinking? Yet, what did it matter if Taylor and Karen not only hit it off but fell in love? That shouldn't concern me, and I hated that the thought bothered me. I grasped for anything to change the subject. "Tell me more about your school,"

"I like school. It's cool." She laughed. "I made a rhyme."

"Do you like poetry?"

"I like some stuff, like *The Midnight Ride of Paul Revere.*"

"Oh, I used to like that one, too."

"It's really like a story, you know. Some of the other poetry we have to study is awfully hard to understand."

"So you enjoy stories. You must like to read."

"My great-grandmother gave me a set of Nancy Drew mysteries, and they're okay, but I prefer the Harry Potter books and the ones about vampires. I'm not allowed to watch television after seven o'clock, so reading is all there is to do before I go to bed. That and homework."

Even though in a way I hated to think anything good about the woman, I couldn't help feeling that Karen Vale was a wise mother to restrict Kimberly's television watching. Someone called it the official Gross—meaning disgusting—National Product.

"She sends me to my room to read or do homework, so she can be with her friends downstairs and not be interrupted."

She looked down at her plate and frowned. "Of course, she doesn't have friends over every night. She does it mostly on weekends. Sometimes one of them will stay overnight. She doesn't think I know that, but I do."

So, to my continuing discomfort, the subject had returned to her mother after all. Maybe the friend who stayed over was a woman, but somehow I didn't think so. I saw a sad look in Kimberly's eyes and patted her hand.

Regardless of what Karen was like at home, she was there in Rome at the moment, sitting next to Taylor in the restaurant, leaning close to him, touching him, and occasionally whispering something in his ear.

As I watched the two of them from across the long table, I couldn't help wishing he were talking to me, explaining something about Rome to me, making *me* laugh at his funny stories.

As it turned out, I hadn't long to wait. When we started our trek back to the hotel, Taylor caught up with me and took my hand. "Hi."

"Hi, yourself." The jealousy I'd been feeling melted, but I didn't know what to say.

"Enjoy the dinner?"

"Yes, very much. Did you?"

"It was great. Especially those little shrimp appetizers."

"What shrimp appetizers?"

"You know, those little brown things they served

first."

"I didn't know they were shrimp. I remember they were crispy."

"Well, maybe not shrimp. Some kind of baby seafood they fried with the legs, antennae and shell still on."

I stopped walking and turned to face him. "Are you telling me I ate something with antennas?"

He looked unhappy that he'd told me. "Well, maybe not, but they were good, whatever they were."

I swallowed. "I'm glad I didn't know all that at the time."

He laughed. "What do they say, 'When in Rome...'"

He squeezed my hand, and I noticed we'd fallen quite a bit behind the rest of the group.

"Should we catch up to them? I don't want to get lost again."

"You won't. Remember I know my way around."

"That's right." I relaxed and slowed my steps even more. I really had no desire to get closer to Karen Vale and let her monopolize Taylor again as she had at dinner. If anyone was going to monopolize him, I decided, it would be yours truly.

"How about some gelato?" he said suddenly.

"We just had dessert. Are you sure you want gelato?"

"Absolutely." He grinned and led me to a nearby corner, and we went down a narrow street until we once again stood in front of a gelato shop. That time I had the peach flavor.

We ate our gelato slowly, walked even more slowly,

and talked about our food likes and dislikes. Like many men, he liked most foods and was willing to try anything new.

"Is there anything you don't like?" I asked.

"I'm not crazy about cooked carrots and some kinds of cheese."

He reminded me of one of my frequent *faux pas*. "I know what you mean. Once, at a fancy buffet given by a big insurance company executive, I took a large bite of what I thought was a little cream puff stuffed with cheese, and it turned out to be hotter than Jalapeno peppers."

"What did you do?"

"I wanted to spit it out, but just then the wife of the host came up to talk to me, so I couldn't."

"Then what?"

"Well, I thought the thing would dissolve in my mouth and I'd just have to live with the taste, but it didn't. So there I was trying to smile at the woman with this thing bobbing on my tongue."

Taylor chuckled, like he thought that was terribly funny.

"So I finally had to spit it out in my napkin, but there were no waste containers anywhere in the room. So I had to put it on one of those little plates where it looked really gross."

"I think you probably did the right thing."

"I mean it wasn't my fault they had no waste baskets."

"Probably they didn't want people putting their good china and silverware in them."

"The wife of the host gave me dirty looks the rest

of the night."

"Is that all?"

"And I didn't get invited back the next year."

"Who needs to go to cocktail parties anyway? You stand around holding a cold glass until your fingers get numb and drop cracker crumbs all over your tie."

"You're just saying that to make me feel better."

He shrugged. "Well, I'm told a lot of business gets conducted at cocktail parties, so I guess they have their uses."

"You're right, but in my case, I tend to eat what's not on anyone's healthy diet and gain two pounds that I can't lose after a month of broiled chicken and skim milk."

He laughed again and swung my free hand like we were a couple of children.

When we finally got to my hotel room door, I confess I was hoping he'd kiss me, but he didn't. I couldn't help but wonder what was going on. Was he more interested in Karen and just spending a little time with me to keep people from figuring it out? Or vice versa? Or did he not really like women at all?

By this time I thought he should have tried to hit on me. Regardless of the reason he didn't, my ego was suffering. I thought of all the other times he seemed to be hiding something, and suddenly I didn't want to know what it might be.

I said, "Good night," and Taylor backed away and bowed like a Musketeer in the old historical drama films, sweeping his hand across his body, as if wielding a plumed hat. "As you wish, milady."

I had to laugh at that, but I did a not-very-good

imitation of a curtsy.

"Until the morrow." He bowed again and backed all the way down the hall to the elevator.

I watched him enter the elevator, his light hair becoming almost golden under the lights, and the distance making him resemble a young Robert Redford. As I closed my door, I realized that—no matter what his preference, Karen, me, or the van driver—I liked having Taylor on the tour.

Chapter 9

I awoke the next morning with immediate thoughts of Taylor. Our walk and conversation after dinner meant a lot to me. I felt valued, as a person he wanted to spend some time with, to get to know. I certainly wanted to know more about him. In spite of my doubts the night before, I especially wanted to know what secret he seemed to be concealing.

After breakfast, I joined Enza and the others in the hotel lobby to wait for the van to take us to San Clemente church. When nine-thirty came and went, and the van still hadn't arrived, Enza used her cell phone to contact the driver. After she finished her conversation with him, she turned to us.

"Our driver is delayed. How do you say it? Stuck in traffic? There is a marathon today with many runners, and several streets are blocked off, so he can't reach us until much later. We will have to go by taxi."

After another delay, two taxis arrived at the curb.

Karen Vale stayed close to Taylor, but after he helped her and Kimberly into the first taxi, he stepped aside and insisted that the Parkers get in with them. As the taxi pulled away, I couldn't help noticing Karen's expression. She'd been outfoxed.

I got into the next taxi, along with the Waxmans,

Enza, and Taylor. I decided that, if Taylor did that deliberately, he must prefer my company to Karen's, but I felt like a high school girl again, looking for signs that some boy liked me. I knew I should have stayed above that sort of thing.

The taxi driver did his best to skirt the marathon runners—at least fifty slender young people dressed in colorful shorts and tee-shirts with numbers on the back—and we made good time. When we arrived at last at the church, we met another tour guide. The sixtyish distinguished-looking gentleman sported a gray beard and was probably a retired professor hired to explain what we'd see that day.

San Clemente church was a Baroque basilica, but its prominence came from the fact that in the nineteenth century excavators discovered the remnants of earlier churches underneath.

As we navigated the narrow staircases and corridors leading down to the earlier excavated sites, I marveled at mosaics and frescoes still visible on floors and walls. I also wondered how those early Christians kept their faith in spite of Rome's efforts to eradicate them. Taylor kept close to me and took my elbow from time to time to keep me from stumbling on the uneven stone floors.

"Apparently an even lower level still exists," he told me.

"I know they call Rome the Eternal City, and I'm beginning to see what they mean."

Taylor agreed with me. "Yes, Italians live with structures from its founding, through the Middle Ages, the Renaissance, and right up to today. At home, we tear down some old buildings when we ought to consider them part of our history."

"I think they call that progress." I allowed some irony to creep into my voice.

He gave a little chuckle as if he appreciated it.

Back outdoors once more, the tour guide instructed us to follow him, and we walked down narrow streets until the Colosseum loomed before us.

I stopped to stare. "It's right here."

"What did you expect?"

"Well, I imagined it off a ways from the city, on a hill, perhaps, surrounded by lawns or just open space. Instead, it's right downtown. The street goes around it, with cars, trucks and buses."

"I told you the Romans live with their history all around them." He seemed about to say more, but just then Karen and Kimberly descended on us.

Kimberly clutched Taylor's sleeve. "Can we go inside?"

"Of course. Why not?"

"I don't know. I just thought— well— I've seen pictures and read about it in school. I mean, it's so famous."

Karen captured Taylor's arm and, once more relegated to Kimberly's side, I followed them toward the doorway which was the entrance. As we walked, I stared up at the enormous outside circle with its familiar arched openings in the walls. They rose in some places to sixty feet or more, while others were lower, where time, weather and, perhaps vandals, had eroded them.

As a tour group, we didn't have to pay the

admission price but proceeded inside the giant structure behind Enza and the guide. My first sight was of wooden flooring that partially covered part of an immense system of catacombs below the main level. The guide told us that what we saw below was the underground temporary home for the animals, slaves and criminals who were sacrificed there.

"This is not the original floor," he explained. "This surface has been built for tourists to walk on. The word 'arena' is Latin for 'sand,' and the entire floor was covered in sand to soak up the blood from the thousands of animals that were killed in the circus."

Once more, Kimberly voiced her opinion. "Ugh, how gross!"

"Did they really send Christians to the lions here?" Karen asked.

"The early Christians were killed in other places as well, but some probably died here too. Since they were considered criminals, they were expendable and provided entertainment to the spectators by fighting animals or gladiators." The guide paused and then made an attempt to be relevant. "They didn't have humane methods in those days: no guillotine, electric chair or lethal injection."

Silent, my body suddenly cold, I thought of those martyrs. Were some of them offered leniency if they renounced Christ? If I lived back then, would I have died for my belief?

"How easily we take freedom of worship for granted," I said.

Taylor drew me aside. His voice soothing, as if he'd been reading my thoughts. "Not to worry. The

Christians got their revenge. Today the whole country looks like a monument to Christianity, with hundreds of churches, cathedrals, and religious art."

While Karen talked to the guide, Taylor took my hand, and we climbed huge stone steps that led to the seats that had been occupied by spectators at the games.

When we'd climbed so high up that the people on the wooden floor looked like ants, he stopped. "Let me take your picture."

"Oh, yes, please. I may want to show someone I really stood inside the Colosseum." If no one else, there was always my boss, who might need to be convinced I hadn't boarded the wrong flight and ended up in Brazil.

I handed my camera to Taylor, and, after using it, he took several more with his own camera.

"Would you like me to take one of you?"

"By all means."

After I snapped it, I said, "Come to think of it, you probably already have lots of pictures of this place because you've been here before."

"That's true." He grinned. "But if you take one of me, you'll have to send me a copy, and we can keep in touch."

"Maybe I'll just do that." In spite of my doubts of the night before, I knew I wanted to keep in touch with him. Yet people who meet on vacation trips often exchange addresses and say things like, "If you ever get to— wherever— be sure to look me up." But it rarely happens.

I enjoyed Taylor's company, and, if he ever did get to Los Angeles, I'd be thrilled to show him around to thank him for his kindness to me on this trip. Oh, sure. The truth was I'd begun to think in larger terms, like maybe a meaningful relationship. I told myself not to laugh. It could happen.

"I'm serious," Taylor said. "Just because we're on a tour in a strange country doesn't mean our friendship has to end when the tour ends." He took my hand and I felt the strength in his palm and long fingers surrounding mine. "I mean it. If we met anywhere, I'd still want to see you more and get to know you better."

My brain seemed to go into a coma, and I couldn't think of anything clever or witty to say. "You're right. People have to meet somewhere. It would be a dull world if we were restricted to whoever happened to live next door to us."

Taylor suddenly frowned and withdrew his hand. What had I said that caused that? He hadn't been in his mysterious mode lately, but there it was again, a sudden look of pain. Why?

Would I ever find out what lay behind it?

Chapter 10

Karen and Kimberly had apparently seen Taylor and me climbing the steps and followed us. Karen soon stood at our side, a bit breathless from the steep climb.

"Here you are. Isn't this a fabulous view?" She didn't wait for a reply. "I see you've been taking pictures. Would you take a picture of Kimberly and me together?"

"Of course." Taylor gave his own camera to me to hold and took Karen's for the pictures. He took two, from different angles, getting different views in the background.

Kimberly, once the snaps were taken, headed off on her own, climbing still higher across the large stone seats.

Karen finally glanced in my direction. "Oh, be a dear and look after her, won't you? I'm quite out of breath." She opened her jacket collar and waved a hand across her throat, as if enticing air to cool her flushed face and neck.

I felt the gesture revealed more bare skin than necessary and then decided I should be ashamed of my unkind thoughts. Yet could she, just once, act like I existed in my own right, not just some annoying excess baggage hanging around Taylor?

Karen touched Taylor's arm again. "Kim is such a sweet child, never gives me a moment's trouble."

Oh yeah? Then why was I supposed to keep an eye on her?

Trying for patience, I took off after the girl, catching up with her a few minutes later. Kim pulled out her own small camera and took a picture of me. "If you give me your address, I can send you one."

"Fine. We'll do that later, shall we? I think we ought to find the tour guide now."

As we climbed back down, Kim took my hand. "I want us to be friends."

"So do I."

She stopped for a moment. "My mother wants to be friends with Mr. Mitchell."

I detected a bit of displeasure in her tone. "Isn't that all right with you? I thought you liked him."

"I do, but he seems to like you more than he likes her." That time, instead of displeasure, her voice held a note of understanding.

Before answering, I tried to define what Kim meant. Sometimes young girls meant more than "like" in using the word, more in the realm of "boyfriend." I didn't think Taylor showed anything as strong as that, see-sawing as he seemed to do between her mother and me, but I could hope, couldn't I? Meanwhile I had to respond to Kimberly. "Can't he like both of us, all of us?"

"My mother doesn't think so."

"What do you mean?"

"Well, when Mr. Mitchell is with you, she gets all kind of funny, you know, jealous like."

I felt myself stiffen. Even if Taylor were beginning to prefer me—and it certainly seemed that way—I didn't need to be in the middle of a possible romantic triangle. "Tell your mother there's nothing between Mr. Mitchell and me. He's just being friendly and helpful to someone who's traveling alone."

She sounded dejected. "I will, but she never listens to me."

Out of the Colosseum finally, we walked through the remains of the Roman Forum, with its ruins of ancient temples, columns and arches. I deliberately avoided being close to Taylor, hoping, if Kim was right, to squelch Karen's jealousy. However, I couldn't help overhearing his explanations to her. She asked dozens of questions, as if he must know more than the guide. She frequently clutched his arm. At times she walked so close to him she hardly let light come between them.

She swept one arm about in a wide circle, and, as usual, spoke loud enough for me to hear. "How old is all this?"

Kimberly, who had been running ahead, came back to Taylor's side to ask her own question. "Is that one of the seven hills of Rome that we read about in school?" She pointed.

"You'll have to ask the guide, but I think that one in front is called Palatine Hill. Wealthy Romans built their luxurious houses there, and that's where the name 'palace' came from."

"Oh, wow." Kim stopped and pulled out her notebook to scribble something in it.

A few paces behind, I waited until Taylor and Karen had walked on before coming abreast of the girl. "I see you're making notes about everything you see."

"Not everything, but I'll bet none of my friends

know where the word 'palace' came from. Or the word 'arena.'" She put her little book away. "I've seen you taking notes sometimes too."

"Not for my friends. I'm here on assignment to write an article."

"Oh, wow, you're a reporter. Did you always want to do that?"

"I always wanted to write, if that's what you mean. Last night you said you like stories. Is writing stories the kind of career you'd like?"

"I'm not sure. They try to make us decide when we're still in middle school so we know what to take in high school, so we—"

I finished for her, "—know what to major in at college." We laughed together.

"I mean, I'm not even fourteen yet. How can I decide now what I should do for the rest of my life?"

"I understand, but don't let that bother you. Even if you pick something and later find you like something else better, you can always change your mind." I thought of Karen. "What does your mother do? Maybe you'd enjoy that too."

She grimaced in disgust, her tone mocking. "Like never in a million years. She works for a plastic surgeon, who helps all those dumb women get their noses fixed, or their boobs lifted."

Before I could comment, Kim dashed off to explore another ruined temple. I lagged behind. Although wearing the heaviest shoes I'd brought on the trip, they were no match for the uneven ground with its occasional paving left over from an earlier millennium. I sighed with relief when we finally climbed a hill and reached the street where a regular sidewalk with smooth pavement took over. Shortly afterward, our van picked us up there for the return to the hotel.

Too tired to try to find a place for a late lunch, I asked room service to bring up a sandwich. Afterward, finished with writing my notes for the day, I lay across the bed. My phone rang.

Taylor. "Robin and Lance Waxman are celebrating their tenth day of marriage and they've asked us to join them at dinner tonight."

"Us?"

"Like everyone else, they seem to think we're a couple. I told them we'd just met, but you need to come along in order to make it a foursome. Odd numbers are so hard to deal with."

I chuckled at his comment. Another dinner with Taylor sounded like a nice idea, but what about Karen and Kimberly Vale?

Taylor had apparently solved that problem already. "We're meeting in the Waxmans' room at seven and we'll all sneak out together." He paused. "They know Karen Vale has been, well, it's pretty obvious, isn't it? So, we'll just slip out discreetly."

Besides the opportunity to spend more time with Taylor, I felt relieved to know that he preferred my company to Karen's. Besides, I wanted to get to know Robin and Lance better. So far on the tour, they'd kept excessively close to each other, holding hands, or otherwise touching, even stopping for a quick kiss. I remembered the early days of my first crush on a boy. We had been like that too.

However, college and working had brought

different expectations. The men I dated were— well, men, not boys. Holding hands and kissing didn't satisfy them. To say nothing of the present culture of television and movies that made it look as if everyone had sex all the time. Sometimes I got tired of explaining why my answer was always "No." Actually I memorized a dozen different ways of turning them down without hurting their feelings or sounding like something out of a Jane Austen novel.

The more I thought about it, the more I realized I felt quite content to be who I was. All I needed was for men to be a bit more— well— more like Taylor. He hadn't tried to take advantage of me in any way. No groping. No suggestive remarks.

Hmmm. Last night I wondered why he hadn't tried any of those things. Like a line from an old movie, if a guy didn't occasionally at least try to make out with me, I felt like saying, "Why? Was I so unattractive, so distant?" This time I appreciated the restraint.

His words of the night before came back to me. He'd said he wanted to see me again, but then, I apparently said something that brought an unpleasant memory, and he changed. So, those perhaps-exchanged photos notwithstanding, Taylor and I might never meet again after the tour ended. Perhaps he recognized that starting a relationship that might have no future would only end up causing pain. Perhaps he felt that if he could never be serious about me, he didn't want to escalate our relationship. In a way that was, well, gallant, and I admired him for it.

He would go to Lake Como and take pictures to paint and sell in art galleries. I would go back home, write up my article and wait for the next assignment. In no time at all, we'd forget each other.

Well, maybe not. That night we'd be together, *sans* Karen and Kimberly, and maybe we'd build a relationship that would last longer than the tour. Unless, of course, there were skeletons in his closet, and I'd inadvertently remind him of them by some stupid remark I might utter. Foot-in-mouth was a disease I could be poster-girl for.

Why was I thinking like that anyway? We would not be alone that evening; Robin and Lance would be there. We would be four people having dinner and talking in generalities. Perhaps Taylor had nothing to do with my being invited. Perhaps the Waxmans didn't want to include Karen, because they'd have to add Kimberly and that would make an uneven number. See, I could rationalize with the best of them.

Chapter 11

I arrived at the Waxmans' hotel room at seven for the planned dinner party, and Lance and Robin greeted me warmly. In fact, Robin hugged me as if we'd known each other since kindergarten instead of a mere three days. I decided she was either one of those people who made friends easily or else was disgustingly happy and needed to spread her joy around.

I had chosen my long, navy-blue skirt and a blue and mauve print blouse, the only dressy outfit I'd packed, which turned out to be appropriate. Robin wore an obviously expensive designer suit of cream silk that almost matched her long, blonde hair, and Lance looked equally well dressed with a blazer over an open-neck shirt into which he'd tucked a colorful ascot. He looked like an actor in one of those British films. Hugh Grant and Jeremy Northam couldn't have looked any better.

True to his word, Taylor, also neatly attired in blazer and slacks but no ascot, arrived moments later.

While Lance offered drinks from a tray he'd apparently ordered from room service, Robin discussed our strategy for avoiding Karen Vale.

She wore a slight frown. "I know I shouldn't feel this way, but it's all too obvious she's making a play for Taylor here, and it's equally obvious, at least to me, that he's not interested but too polite to tell her to buzz off." She turned to Taylor. "Did I get it right?"

Taylor grinned but seemed uneasy.

"I mean," Robin continued, "can't she take a hint? In the common sense department, she's a cross between oatmeal and a hamster."

Lance howled with laughter, but Taylor apparently thought Robin had gone too far. "I don't mind talking to her and answering her questions, but she acts as if I know more than the tour guides, and I don't."

"Have you told her that?" Lance asked.

"Several times. It doesn't seem to faze her." He shrugged.

"And the way she clutches your arm and pulls you close," Robin said, "is rude, at the very least." She emphasized her words with a toss of her head, sending her hair swaying.

I'd have thought Robin was too busy clutching Lance's arm and pulling *him* close so they could embrace and kiss, to have noticed Karen's behavior. They were, after all, on their honeymoon, and a certain amount of koochy-coo on their part was excusable.

"At least for tonight," Robin went on, "you won't have to sit next to her at dinner. If you like," she said to Taylor, "Lance and I can surround you next time so she won't get a chance to monopolize you. Right, Lance?"

"Whatever." He turned to me. "Maybe Sydney should be the one to do that."

"Me?" I protested. "I'm just another tour member. We only met on the plane to Rome the other day."

"Nevertheless—"

Taylor interrupted him, which pleased me, as he seemed as uncomfortable discussing all this as I was.

"Why don't we go on to dinner now?"

We hustled out, and, after the elevator ride to the lobby, we took a taxi to a sprawling restaurant in one of the many squares liberally sprinkled throughout the city. Robin suggested we dine outdoors and, since rain was not expected, we all agreed.

We seated ourselves at a table for four near a boxy hedge that sported a lantern, and Robin said, "I love Italy, but most Italians smoke, and I can't bear to be inside next to a table of smokers. You don't smoke, do you?" She turned to us and frowned, as if suddenly realizing Taylor or I might.

"No," Taylor answered quickly. "I don't, and I don't think Sydney does either." He glanced toward me, and I nodded, although the subject of smoking was something I generally avoided.

"At home, we have non-smoking sections in restaurants," Lance added, but so far, I haven't found one like that here."

"In California," Taylor said, "smoking isn't allowed inside any restaurants." He glanced at me again. "Isn't that so?"

"Yes, not even in bars, I think."

"Really?" Lance asked.

"There we'd have to eat *indoors*, because smoking is allowed in the outdoor sections of restaurants."

"How civilized." After a pause, Robin added, "What are you thinking, Sydney?"

"I often wish those Native Americans had never discovered tobacco and started the, er, habit."

The waiter appeared with menus, and I read mine eagerly, trying to decide what to order, grateful for the chance to forget smoking.

After a moment, Robin said, "I'll have the duck." She put down her menu. "I had a simply divine duck breast in Paris. I hope they make it that well here."

We all decided to try her suggestion, and the waiter left with our orders.

As we waited, Robin returned to the subject of smoking. "Have you never smoked?" she asked Taylor. "Most boys take it up some time when they're young. Lance did at fifteen." She looked at him with a big smile. "Fortunately he gave it up again at sixteen."

"I tried it once," Taylor said, "and got terribly sick."

"I'll bet *you* never did." Robin turned to me again. "I think you started to say, earlier, 'that *filthy* habit.'"

I looked down into my lap and straightened my napkin, embarrassed that I had let my feelings show.

"So what's your story?" Robin looked eager, as if everyone who didn't smoke had to have a story. She leaned across the table, her voice cajoling. "Tell us all the lurid details."

I didn't answer immediately, but something about Robin's look made me decide to tell her. "Smoking killed my brother."

"Oh, I'm sorry— I shouldn't have—" She looked genuinely upset to have opened a painful subject.

I hurried on. "No, it's not what you think. He didn't die because he smoked, because he didn't smoke. He was killed by a drunk driver who ran a red light and broadsided him."

"So where did the smoking come in?" Lance asked.

"The driver had been smoking and dropped his

cigarette in his lap. Between trying to find it, and being rather intoxicated, he lost control of his car."

"Oh, how awful." Robin looked genuinely concerned. "Did the man go to jail for it?"

"Not yet. His trial comes up soon. His lawyer apparently advised him to plead 'not guilty' and let a jury decide."

"But surely there's no doubt that his decisions were what took your brother's life?"

"He said it was an accident. He didn't mean to do it."

"But if he hadn't been drunk—" Lance said. "I mean, I like the occasional glass of wine, but I know when to quit."

Thinking about my brother brought angry tears and I fought to hold them back, but Taylor, apparently sensing my distress, put his hand on mine and gave it a gentle squeeze. Yet, in a way I felt relieved. The tragedy also explained why I lost any desire to drink alcohol.

"I don't blame you for hating smokers," Robin said.

I wanted to say that I didn't hate anyone, but the waiter brought our salads and bread, and, although I enjoyed the feel of his palm against mine, I reluctantly withdrew my hand from Taylor's in order to pick up my fork.

Lance brought the subject back to food. "Even if they don't prepare the duck exactly like the French do, I think Italian food is very good, don't you?"

"Yes," Taylor agreed. "It's excellent."

"So what do you do? Are you in business?"

We spent the next hour enjoying the meal and discussing what everyone did for a living. Lance was vice president of a bank he and a friend opened two years earlier in a Chicago suburb.

Robin had been a model and intended to continue that career. "Until I get too old and fat, or have a baby. Whichever comes first." She leaned close to Lance and grinned up at him. "I'm ready whenever you are."

Lance's face flushed momentarily. "So I've noticed."

Robin's giggle trilled in the night air, and she turned to Taylor and me. "Please excuse us, but we are on our honeymoon and, as you can tell, very much in love."

"So I've noticed," Taylor said, repeating Lance's words, and Robin laughed again, making nearby diners look our way and smile indulgently.

Robin suddenly looked across the table at Taylor and me. "Have you ever been married?"

"No," Taylor answered.

"How about you, Sydney?"

"No."

Robin looked thoughtful. "I don't know if that's good or bad. On the one hand—"

Taylor interrupted her. "In my case, it's probably good. I travel half the year, and I'd either have to leave my family behind or drag them along, which would probably play havoc with any children's education."

"Not if you traveled abroad. They'd see all these great sights and maybe even become multi-lingual. It could be a real advantage." Holding her fork in mid-air, she looked at me. "How about you?"

"I travel for my job too, and I'd hate having to leave a husband behind for long periods of time." Still, I thought our responses sounded more like excuses than reasons.

The subject closed when the waiter brought a tray with a bill to the table.

Lance reached for it immediately. "Oh, by the way, "I forgot to tell you before, but you're our guests tonight."

"That's not necessary," Taylor said. "Just because we chose to eat together."

"No, I'm serious. As I told you, we're celebrating." He looked fondly at Robin for a moment. "Besides, my parents are filthy rich, and they're paying for everything." He shrugged.

Taylor grinned. "How did you manage to be born to rich parents?"

"I put in an order, of course." He laughed.

"Why didn't I think of that?"

"Oh well," Lance said, "your parents may not have had gobs of money, but I'm sure they had some other good qualities."

I looked at Taylor, but he only revealed a tight smile and a crease furrowed his forehead. He didn't answer. Once more, I wondered if he harbored a secret.

We walked back to the hotel, Taylor assuring us it wasn't far and that he knew the way.

"Good idea," Lance said. "We can walk off that dinner. I'm afraid I eat too much when I'm on vacation."

"I'll put you on a diet when we get home." Robin hugged his arm to her side and nestled her head against his chest.

I felt a bit like a *voyeur* to their intimacy, but, on the other hand, Robin and Lance didn't seem to require privacy or to care if people noticed their attentions to each other. Taylor, however, merely took my arm from time to time, helping me when we crossed rough pavement or encountered curbs.

In the hotel lobby, we waited for the elevator, and Robin thanked us for joining their celebration. "It was super getting to know you both." She threw her arms around me in a tight hug, then let me go and did the same to Taylor. The men didn't hug. Instead, they grabbed each other's arms and patted backs. Then we all squeezed into the little elevator and the men punched the buttons for their floors.

As the elevator groaned its way up, Robin said, "We must do this again in Florence and then again in Venice." The elevator stopped, and she grinned and waved before getting off and skipping down the hallway.

On my floor, Taylor once again took my key and unlocked the door. Then he turned, put his arms around me and pressed me to him. Almost immediately, he released me and backed away.

"That Robin is quite a character."

"I like her."

"Oh, I do too." He paused and cleared his throat. "So demonstrative." He moved closer. "I felt as if I might betray her spirit if I didn't hug you."

I had enjoyed the brief moment in his arms, feeling their strength, smelling his aftershave and the faint scent of his woolen jacket. "It's okay." Thinking of

Karen Vale, I almost added. "But I don't think we should make it a habit in public," but I didn't.

Taylor looked uncomfortable. He finally said, "Good night" and walked toward the elevator. I went inside and closed the door. I had enjoyed the evening and especially that brief last-minute hug.

I undressed for bed but couldn't sleep. I kept remembering what I'd said about my brother's death. I should never have mentioned it. I knew I shouldn't hate anyone, but I found it difficult not to hate the man who—through stupidity and carelessness—had killed him. And I could do nothing except show up at his trial and make sure he didn't get off lightly. I wiped away the angry tears that ran down my face, but the images that had been evoked refused to go away so easily. In my mind's eye, I went back more than a year in time.

There were six of us in those days—father, mother, my older brother and sister, then me and my younger brother, Howard. Howard was only eighteen, just about to graduate from high school. He was handsome, smart, and so good at sports that he played both basketball and baseball and was captain of the swim team. He was on his way home from a date when the drunken driver hit him.

I had moved to L.A. by that time and worked for a small newspaper, as well as writing freelance magazine articles on the side. I was working there when I got the telephone call about Howard. I came home at once, and there I stayed for three months. I felt closer to Howard than to my older brother and sister, probably because we were the pranksters in the family. We played practical jokes and livened up the dinner-table conversation with funny anecdotes. We both seemed to find amusing things in life to call attention to and joke about.

So I grieved, I mean, really grieved. I couldn't eat, couldn't sleep, cried all the time, never went out, and seldom even combed my hair. Finally my father took the family aside and did what they called an "intervention." They do this, I'm told, for people who abuse alcohol or drugs, trying to get them into rehab centers for help. In my case, my family just wanted to tell me I had to return to the land of the living.

My father spoke first. "We all love you, and your ever-present grief hurts the rest of us, making us sad for you and keeping the household in a perpetual state of, well, like suspended animation. When will it end?"

Mother spoke about needing to heal our wounds, especially emotional ones. She said that despite the cruel accident which took Howard from us at such a young age, until we died, we might never know why certain things happened.

My older brother complained that my attitude made him feel guilty. "You're not the only one who loved him, you know. It's not fair to expect us to stop living just because you choose to become a martyr about this."

Jennifer said, "Howard would have wanted you to get on with your life, to do something more worthwhile than wasting away like this."

There was more which I no longer remember, but that was sufficient to break what I began to realize was my self-absorption. The intervention lasted all day, and at the end we were all exhausted, and bleary-eyed from crying, but hugging one another. I thanked them, went to my room and soon fell asleep. I woke up later with a strong desire to give myself permission to get back into the game. I had to stop looking like someone from a remake of *Grapes of Wrath*.

I cleaned up my act, got a haircut and a facial and moved back to the apartment where my roommate did her own share of helping me recover. I didn't promise to forgive the creep who had caused my pain, but I tried to live a life--as much as my unpredictable nature would allow----that Howard might be proud of.

Chapter 12

Day Five

Softly falling rain greeted our tour group the next morning, and I mentally thanked my mother who insisted I always include a raincoat in my travel gear. Since everyone else also showed up with umbrellas or raincoats or both, Enza, whom apparently nothing short of a hurricane could halt, walked us to the Vatican. There we waited in line with hundreds of others until we could enter. Once more, our special guide, the elderly professor, met us and conducted the tour.

Taylor stood in line with me, but after we entered the building, we got separated by the crowds. Actually it was partly my own fault. I'd temporarily misplaced the ticket Enza had given me while we stood in line. Aware of its importance, I'd tucked it in the outside pocket of my purse, and then, naturally, when I emptied the contents of the inside of the purse onto the ticket-taker's counter—which didn't go over well with him—it didn't drop out.

Enza came to my rescue, but by that time some coins and my lipstick had rolled off the man's tiny table—it wasn't my fault that they didn't provide him with a decent-sized table—and while I was trying to pick them all up, a line of grumblers grew behind me.

However, in a torrent of Italian, it didn't take Enza long to persuade the obstinate ticket-taker that I was part of her special tour group and he should let me in, ticket or not. Even so, the rest of our party was scattered well ahead of us, and Karen had, of course, used my temporary absence to pounce on Taylor again.

Hours later, after walking through countless corridors and museums filled with religious art, we finally reached the Sistine Chapel. As in the case of the Colosseum, I'd been looking forward to seeing it, especially Michelangelo's famous painting of God's finger touching Adam's finger. The cloudy day made it quite dim inside, and when I finally stood in the chapel I couldn't find the painting right away.

My head tilted up, I searched for several minutes among the many paintings covering the ceiling before I saw the right image. Kimberly, who had found me a few minutes earlier and stood at my side, craned her neck upward as well. "Is that the one?" She pointed with her right hand.

"Yes, that must be. I don't see anything else that looks like it."

"But it's so small."

I tried to put a positive spin on it. "If the ceiling weren't so high it would probably look larger."

"But it's no bigger than the others. My guidebook is full of stuff about it. I thought it would be huge."

"So did I." There always seemed so much emphasis on that image, that I, too, expected a gigantic painting, perhaps even the size of a mural.

"That one on the back wall." Kimberly pointed. "What's that called?"

"The Last Judgment."

"Now *that's* really big. How come nobody talks about that one?"

"I guess some do. Our guide mentioned it, remember?" I patted her arm. "Are you very disappointed?"

Kim shrugged and looked away. "Well, duh. It's a major nothing."

Trying to hide my own disappointment, I followed Kimberly and the rest of the crowd of tourists into St. Peter's Cathedral. The guide had a lot to say about the dome, the altars and the many statues, and, like everyone else, I suppose, I was impressed with its grandeur. Except for one altar which looked as if it were made out of old brown wood someone had rescued from a fire. But then, I'm not a Catholic, so what do I know? When we went outdoors at last, I found the rain had stopped.

I took pictures of the Colonnade and especially the obelisk that Caligula brought back from Egypt.

Kim read aloud from her guidebook. "It says here that the Egyptian Pharoah Akhnaton gave the idea of one God to Moses."

"Do you go to church or Sunday School and learn about God?"

"No. I have a friend who goes all the time, and she loves her Sunday school. Sometimes she tells me about the stories they read from the Bible."

"You said before that you like stories. Do you like the ones from the Bible?"

"Yeah." She paused. "When we were in the Colosseum yesterday I remembered one. It was about when Daniel was put in a lion's den, but the lions didn't hurt him because he believed in God." She looked up at me. "How come the lions ate other Christians if they all believed in God?"

"I don't know. Maybe some weren't eaten. I think I read that many were spared, especially the ones who fought gladiators. If they fought well, sometimes the emperor would let them live."

"I guess that's true. After all, if they were *all* killed, there wouldn't have been any left to start the churches."

Since Kimberly seemed satisfied with her own conclusion, I didn't say any more. Who was I to talk about it anyway? I took a Comparative Religion class in college but remembered only a smattering of what we were taught, mainly that there were many different religions, all of which were convinced theirs was the only true one. Unfortunately, that fact usually resulted in some believers doing nasty things to non-believers.

"Did you take enough pictures?" I asked her.

Before she could answer, I heard Karen's voice calling, "Kimberly, come here, sweetie."

Kim sighed. "My mother thinks I spend too much time with you." She shrugged, said a swift goodbye and hurried to obey.

Could the woman's attitude be more annoying? First she insisted on my playing nursemaid to her daughter—no doubt so she could flirt with Taylor without interference—and now she was apparently jealous of Kim's relationship with me.

As for Taylor, at first I'd been thinking he might have some terrible secret to hide, but why? He'd been nothing but polite, helpful and sympathetic. More than that, for the first time ever, I thought I might have met my Mr. Right. I hoped he liked me too, and, especially after the brief hug he'd given me the night before, I even began to entertain the possibility something would come of it. Then I figuratively smacked myself upside the head. I lived in Los Angeles, and Taylor lived in Phoenix and traveled a lot. Long distance relationships never worked out.

Just as I was squelching romantic thoughts about him, Taylor himself appeared, and together we walked back toward the street where the van would be waiting to pick us up.

"I enjoyed last night, but I was sorry to hear about your brother."

"Thanks. I probably ought to apologize to the Waxmans for telling about what happened to him. I hope I didn't spoil the evening for everyone."

"I get the impression nothing spoils Robin's enthusiasm for life."

"That's a great quality to have."

"I think you have it too. Until last night, I never would have guessed there was such an unhappy event in your past."

Feeling very close to him by then, I told him the whole story, intervention and all. "So now you know, and I promise not to talk about it again. I'm pretty much over it. I don't know why I brought it up last night."

"As I remember, Robin pressed you about smoking. Certain topics can often trigger unwanted memories."

"What about you?"

"What *about* me?"

"I'd like to know more about you. The other night I asked if you had any brothers or sisters, and you never answered me."

"Really? Well, I'm sorry. I'll answer it now. No, I never had any. I was an only child."

I persisted. "But there was something else, too. Last night when Lance suggested your parents had good qualities even if they didn't have lots of money, you didn't answer him. You looked, well, sad." Sad wasn't exactly the right word but it sounded safer.

"I didn't mean to."

"Are your parents living? Are they okay?"

"Yes, they're fine." He rubbed his chin. "Look, I don't mean to sound secretive or rude, but I'd rather not talk about them if you don't mind."

"No, you're not being rude, but I can't rule out secretive."

He stopped walking, took my hand and turned me about so we were face to face, only inches apart. "I like you so much, and I feel you'd understand, but— well, it's a long, involved story, and I just can't talk about it now. Maybe later, okay?"

"Okay, whatever you say."

We resumed walking, this time hand in hand, which, along with his having said he liked me very much, made me extremely happy. I looked around, almost hoping to see Karen, hoping she'd notice my hand in Taylor's. Boy, was that juvenile, or what? Like high school kids going "Nyaa, nyaa."

That night the entire tour group had dinner together again, and as usual, Karen managed to sit next to Taylor. I did my best to prevent it happening, but—unless I wanted to look as aggressive as she did—I couldn't stop her. So I made small talk with Kimberly on one hand and Enza on the other. It was pleasant, and I learned a lot more about Rome from Enza. But my hormones were calling for Taylor, and apparently his hormones weren't listening. After dinner we said our "good nights" and went to our separate rooms.

However, a little bit later, Taylor knocked on my door and we took a late walk along the Tiber River that runs through part of Rome. He told me tales of the ghetto that once existed near the bend of the river.

"So there were Jews living here?"

"Oh, yes, they've been here since the time of Pompey when they were brought here as slaves. Later they helped to finance the career of Julius Caesar, and he let them follow their own religion and indulge in certain kinds of trade."

"What else used to be here?"

"There's still a hospital on Tiber Island, but long before that there were theaters. Early emperors imported classical Greek drama, but later they degenerated into music hall shows with naked women and lots of violence. Condemned criminals were sometimes actually butchered on stage."

I raised my hand. "Stop! I don't want to know about that. It was bad enough learning what used to go on in the Colosseum."

"Yes, it was grisly, and I think it just shows that man's inhumanity to man has existed for a long time."

"I'm glad we don't do those awful things anymore."

"Maybe we're learning." He shrugged, and I could tell he wasn't convinced by his own words.

I didn't want to dwell on such things. The trees along the river were beautiful, lights shown from buildings, and the air felt warm and balmy. I put my hand in Taylor's, and we walked back to the hotel in silence. At my door, he kissed me on the forehead before leaving for his own room.

Okay, the kiss on the forehead was not exactly the one I'd been hoping for, but it was a start. First he held my hand a long time, then he'd hugged me and now the kiss on the forehead. With luck, maybe next time he'd aim lower. I smiled in the dark.

Chapter 13

Day Six

Early the next morning, I ate a lovely breakfast in the dining room and packed my bag for the trip to Florence. I hoped to sit with Taylor in the van, but—although I thought he seemed eager to sit with me again—it didn't happen. Instead, after I took a seat, Kimberly rushed in and sat next to me, and I didn't have the heart to tell her I preferred someone else. Besides, it was only a short trip. Taylor waited until everyone boarded and then sat alone in one of the five empty seats in the back.

When we left the city behind, Kim asked if she could have the window seat, and I obliged. Enza, on the special reversed seat in front, faced the rest of her charges and explained we would travel on a modern highway that ran all the way from Naples in the south to Milan in the north. Using a map, she talked about Tuscany, the area of Italy we traveled through. Part of her job, no doubt, but I felt as if I were being lectured to and hoped there wouldn't be a quiz later.

When we stopped for a coffee break at a combination gas station, cafe and mini grocery store, Kimberly remained close to me and asked me to help her find the bathrooms. "How do you know where to go?"

"See that sign, W.C.? That stands for 'water closet.' It's what the British call a toilet."

"The British?"

"Yes, Britons have been coming to Tuscany for hundreds of years. I suppose the sign was because the Italians wanted to make them feel at home. Don't you remember we heard Enza say that?"

"I was looking out the window. The countryside is beautiful. I saw lots of flowers."

I managed to get fruit juice for both of us, and we shared a tiny table next to a window. "I thought your mother didn't want you to spend so much time with me."

"Oh, she's very inconsistent." Kim grinned, as if proud of having used a long word correctly. "Anyway, it was my idea this time. I figured she wouldn't make a fuss on the van in front of everybody."

"Well, I enjoy your company."

Kim glanced around. "See, there's my mother now, following Mr. Mitchell, as usual."

I didn't want to appear to be spying on them, but, after Kim's comment, I couldn't seem to avoid watching. My face felt warm. "It's not polite to stare." I said it as much to myself as to Kim.

"I know, but she doesn't even notice us anyway."

Before I could comment, Enza called us to return to the van, and we continued our journey to Florence.

As we waited in the hotel lobby for room assignments, Kim asked what "Ponte Vecchio" meant. "I can see it from here and it's some kind of big deal."

"It means 'Old Bridge,' and it's the bridge that spans the Arno River. I think *Ponte* is 'bridge' in Italian and *Vecchio* is 'old.'"

She frowned. "But that makes it 'Bridge Old.' That's backward."

"French is that way, too. The adjective follows the noun instead of preceding it, as we do in English."

Kim shrugged. "Well, it's their language. I guess they can do it that way if they want to."

I laughed, and then Taylor came over to us.

"I heard you talking about the bridge." He turned to Kim. "Do you like jewelry?"

"Well, yeah." Like he'd asked a foolish question.

He pointed out the window. "The bridge is lined with shops. They're all jewelry shops, selling gold and silver jewelry."

Kim looked up at Taylor without speaking, as if waiting for the punch line.

"You might want to take your mother there, ask her to buy a souvenir for you."

Kim's eyes sparkled. "Cool." She hurried away.

Taylor leaned close to me and whispered, "Meet me at Queen Victoria in twenty minutes for lunch."

"What?"

"Turn left when you leave the hotel, and it's in the next block, on the right." He winked and strode away toward the elevator, which bore the British word "Lift" overhead.

I went up in the next elevator and found my room. It almost resembled a suite, with a separate area for a bed, a modern bathroom, plus a sitting room with couch, a desk and a television set. However, the only English language channel was a news program, like CNN, from London. I watched while I unpacked and learned more than I cared to know about what was going on in Bangladesh.

The sun was shining and the weather warm, so I pulled off my blazer and exchanged my white long-sleeved blouse for a pink short-sleeved one.

Twenty minutes later I left the hotel and turned left at the corner. The side street contained shops selling shoes, leather goods, antiques and jewelry. Interspersed were the ever-present pizza and gelato shops. I saw that Queen Victoria—obviously also named to attract British visitors—looked less like my idea of an English pub, and more like the other Italian shops that sold pizza and six kinds of sandwiches.

Taylor stood just inside the entrance and suggested we order the ham and cheese sandwich, which turned out to be in an envelope that resembled pita bread. Then he found a table for two in a back corner, left me there for a moment and returned with two soft drinks, which I assumed were Coke.

After he sat down, I teased him. "I suspect you had an ulterior motive with that jewelry suggestion to Kimberly."

"You guessed right, but how was I ever going to get you alone otherwise?"

I felt a glowing sensation. He wanted to see me as much as I did him. Nevertheless, I felt constrained not to reveal my feelings too much. There was still that "ships that pass in the night" thing to consider.

"I like Kim." I paused while I took a bite from my sandwich. "I've enjoyed talking to her, answering her questions."

"Her mother should be doing that. Not you."

"But one of the pleasures of travel is meeting different people and making new friends."

Taylor sipped his drink. "Personally, I prefer to have a choice in which friends I get to know."

I didn't answer, not wanting to speak ill of Karen Vale, who, I was fairly sure, Taylor meant.

"After the tour this afternoon, we have another free night, and I've asked the Parkers to have dinner with us. Is that all right with you?"

"Of course. I'd like that."

"They're quite a bit older than anyone else on this tour, so I thought we should make them feel included."

"That's very thoughtful."

"Not really. It's just another excuse to be paired with you. I'm hoping a certain person, whose initials are Karen Vale, takes the hint."

"I think you must often find it hard to speak your mind."

"You're right. I've never wanted to be blunt, to hurt people by what I say. Unkind words can never be taken back. They can cause deep wounds on the psyche if not on the flesh."

Once again, I felt he referred to a troubled past. Who had said terrible things to him, the things he hinted at that had made him, in his own words, a loner? Or had he said words he now regretted? Impulsively, I touched his hand where it lay on the small round table. "You're a good person."

He squeezed my hand and his face flushed. "Not really. I fight the devil all the time. Sometimes he wins."

"I don't believe it."

He laughed, breaking the mood. "Tell me about you."

I withdrew my hand. "I'm just ordinary."

"You can't be. Californians are never ordinary."

"That's not true."

"I've spent time in San Francisco, so I know what they're like."

"I don't know who you hung out with, but I assure you we're no different from people in the East or Midwest." I ate the last bite of my sandwich. "Well, perhaps there are a few more, er, colorful folks in San Francisco. But, in spite of what you read in the media, southern Californians are just, you know, normal. Oh, we don't hurry as much as New Yorkers, some of us wear jeans and sneakers to the opera, and we go to the beach a lot, but aside from that..."

"Tell me about your family."

"My father owns a small business making office supplies—folders, labels, forms, things like that."

"What about your mother?"

"She stayed at home while we children were small, then she started writing advertising copy for my dad's business and that escalated into doing the same for some of his customers. She works from home on her computer."

"So your mother is a writer too. That must be where you got your talent for it."

"Perhaps, if I have any talent."

"What about your older brother?"

"Owen is in law school, having finally decided that he was never going to be a big-league baseball player."

He grinned. "And your sister?"

"She was a schoolteacher until she got married. She lives in Texas now and plans to go back to teaching when her own children are older." I held out a hand, palm up. "See, all-American family. Except for my younger brother being killed, nothing unusual ever happened to us. None of us is bizarre."

"But I can't just take your word for it." His lips curved up in a smile and he leaned across the table. "When I come to California in the summer, I'll look you up and see for myself."

I returned his smile. "That would be great."

He took my hand. "I'm looking forward to it already."

I slowly pulled my hand free, finished my drink and changed the subject. "I think it's almost time to meet Enza for the tour."

"We still have another half hour. Why don't we take a little walk and find some gelato to finish off our lunch?"

"Gee." I rose from the chair, remembering all the gelato shops I'd passed. "You think?"

He laughed again and followed me outside. "Turn right. I know just where to go."

Cups filled with lemon gelato in our hands, we strolled down the street, glancing into windows and occasionally going inside a shop to get a better look at a particular vase or framed picture.

"Florence is known for its leather," Taylor told me. "Do you like leather?"

"Only for shoes. I'm not into wearing leather clothes."

"Too hot?"

I frowned. "How about expensive?"

"If I hadn't already told Kimberly to take her mother there, we could go to the jewelry stores on the *Ponte Vecchio* and I could buy something for you."

I stopped walking and turned to him, my voice firm. "No, you couldn't. I don't want you to buy jewelry for me. Or anything else." Realizing how it might sound, I softened my tone. "I mean, I wouldn't feel comfortable accepting gifts from you. I'm glad we're friends, but, well, lunch and gelato are my limit."

"And dinner tonight."

"Only if you insist. After all, I'm on an expense account. My company will pay for the meals that aren't included in the tour package."

"In that case, I accept your offer, but not tonight. You can pay next time. Tonight I'm paying." He turned me about and we retraced our steps to the hotel. "If I don't get a chance to talk to you again, remember I'm picking you up at your door at seven."

Feeling like a conspirator, I nodded. I wished we needn't be so secretive. I wished Karen Vale hadn't decided to make Taylor her conquest *du jour.* Why didn't she take the hints Taylor offered? What was she thinking?

Chapter 14

Enza conducted the afternoon tour herself and it included more walking than I normally did in a week. We crossed the Ponte Vecchio, saw the Pitti Palace, went into another ornate church, and strolled past a large outdoor market filled with vendors selling leather coats, skirts, pants and handbags.

We passed Ferragamo's large building and I almost lost the group while I admired his shoes. They looked elegant with their pointy toes and stiletto heels, and I'd have liked to wear them with one of those fashionable short, flirty skirts. However, I couldn't afford those prices and decided I would have to wait for a knock-off to come to L.A.

Probably not all the other people we saw were tourists, or even British, but there were certainly plenty of them, even more than in Rome. Street traffic was heavy too, with cars and motor scooters zooming by almost constantly.

Kim appeared and walked next to Taylor, sometimes taking his hand and looking up at him as if hanging onto his every word. Karen, who had been not far behind her daughter, hurried up and did the same.

I supposed Karen had instructed Kim to spend more time with Taylor than me, and I tried not to let it bother me. I concentrated on the sights and reminded myself that I'd be with Taylor that night.

* * *

He made reservations at a restaurant Enza had recommended and, together with John and Mary Parker, we walked across the bridge over the Arno River. When we reached our destination and settled at a table, Taylor said, "I hope that wasn't too much walking. We can take a taxi back."

"No," Mary Parker said. "I'm fine. John's older than I am, but he has more stamina. That's not unusual, I guess."

"Men have to be stronger, don't they?" Taylor said. "They hunted and killed animals, while the women stayed in the caves and cooked over an open fire."

"Oh, my," Mary said. "We're not *that* old." We all laughed. "When John came back from the service he got a job as an engineer in an office, not exactly a dangerous occupation."

"You were in the service?" Taylor asked. "Korea?"

"No, World War Two. I'm eighty-five."

"You don't look it." I admired the man's smooth face, twinkling blue eyes and thick, white hair.

"Thank you. I owe it all to growing up on a farm, but nowadays we say, 'good genes.'"

During dinner, Taylor asked John about his experiences during the war, and John said that he fought in Patton's army and helped to liberate Italy. Taylor asked lots of questions about that, and John answered as if the war had been yesterday instead of so many years ago.

"I liked Patton," John said. "He was sometimes

harsh, but always fair. We knew he didn't expect anything of us that he wasn't prepared to do himself. And he was a brilliant strategist."

He paused and a sad look crossed his face. "Afterward I visited a concentration camp. I saw what had happened to those wretched, starved people."

His eyes misted, as if the memory still haunted him, and the rest of us fell silent as well. I wanted to lighten the mood, but for once no quip seemed appropriate, even to me. Then the waiter saved the moment from becoming too gloomy. He slipped and fell, dropped a tray, and the clatter of dishes made everyone in the restaurant jump.

Taylor, like the rest of us, laughed and changed the subject, bringing the conversation from the past to the present, especially the sights we were seeing on the tour.

"I love Italy," Mary Parker said. "It's so beautiful, and the people are friendly."

"And the food is good," John added. He turned to Taylor. "But you've been here before, haven't you?"

"Several times, and for those same reasons."

"What about you?" Mary asked me.

"This is my first trip, but I'm very impressed. The Italians are not only friendly, they're so creative."

"Always have been," John said. "My guide book says there's one piece of art work for every person who lives here. We could never see them all in one lifetime."

"But Enza's working on it," I said. They laughed with me.

"Look at Titian, Bernini, and Michelangelo. What other country has produced so many great artists?"

"Don't forget Leonardo Da Vinci," Taylor said.

"He was an inventor, as well."

"And Galileo." Mary said.

"He wasn't an inventor," Taylor said, "but that counts."

"And then there's music. Where would opera be without Verdi, Puccini, Rossini?"

I added my two cents' worth. "They had writers, too, like Dante and Boccaccio, and even Umberto Eco."

"Oh, my," Mary said. "Is there nothing the Italians aren't good at?"

"Politics," John said. "Prime Ministers change regularly. Maybe it's because they're so creative, they can't be governed."

"Like they say about the French: 'Who can govern a country with three hundred kinds of cheese?'"

We all laughed at that.

"Well, speaking of art," I said, "Taylor's an artist and paints pictures of this beautiful scenery."

"Really?" Mary's eyes lit up.

"I'm not that good." Taylor abruptly changed the subject. "I understand you have a large family. How many children do you have?"

Once more he'd been reluctant to talk about himself. I stared at him, wondering what that was all about. Sure, he hinted at a past. Now he didn't want to talk about the present.

Mary answered, pride in her tone. "Four children, thirteen grandchildren and one great-grandchild."

"I'm impressed. Do your children live near you?"

"One daughter does. The others are scattered. That gives us an excuse to travel a lot. We visit them, usually on our way back from someplace else. I think it's nice that you folks are seeing the world while you're young."

"This is my first trip outside the country, and it's really business," I said.

"Business for me, too," Taylor added.

Mary Parker looked from Taylor to me and back again. "You've never been married?"

"No, never," Taylor said.

"No," I answered as well.

"So you have no children?" She paused. "Excuse me, that may sound strange, but these days people seem to have children without ever having been married."

"No, no children." Then I looked over at Taylor. Was it possible that the secret he said he might share with me had something to do with a child?

But he answered quickly. "No children."

"Forgive me for being a bit nosy," Mrs. Parker said, "but you ought to have them while you're still young, like we did."

"I thought you said we should travel while we're young." Taylor grinned.

"That, too."

John looked at his wife. "Now Mary, you mustn't tell other folks how to run their lives." He turned to Taylor and smiled. "She's very wise—that's why I married her—but she does like to pass her wisdom on, welcome or not."

"I'm sorry." Mary glanced at me. "You told me that you two aren't, well, together, but—"

John interrupted. "She likes to play matchmaker too. She found the girls she thought our boys should marry, and they did marry them, and it worked out beautifully."

"So I think—" Mary began, but again John stopped her with a hand on her arm.

"She thinks you two look like a perfect couple. There, it's said, and now we can forget about it and not embarrass you folks any further."

Taylor and I both laughed with them, but I felt a warm glow at the thought that Mary Parker believed Taylor and I might have a future together. Yet what did Taylor think, and what about his mysterious past? I didn't learn any more, because, once at my door again, he gave me a kiss on the top of my head. This time, before he could retreat to his own room, I pulled his head down and kissed him on the lips.

He looked startled, then pleased, but he joked about it. "Oh, this tour gets more interesting all the time." Holding my hands, he kissed me back, then grinned. "Touché, m'lady. I wonder what tomorrow may bring." So did I, but I let him leave.

Chapter 15

Day Seven

The next morning I saw Taylor with Karen and Kim, so I didn't approach him but stayed close to the day's tour guide, a middle-aged woman wearing no-nonsense shoes and a serious expression. She marched her charges across the bridge and into San Marcos church and monastery where each tiny monk's cell—and there were at least forty of them—was embellished with a religious painting. Then we went to the Academie which housed Michelangelo's statue of David. My heart swelled with gratitude at the thrill of being in the presence of the masterpiece.

The afternoon free, I went shopping for make-up and was directed to a Farmacie which sold reasonably priced Clinique products and where the clerks spoke excellent English.

When I returned to the hotel, I hoped to see Taylor and perhaps take up where we'd left off the night before, but, instead I found Kim waiting for me in the lobby. She grabbed my arm and suggested we go upstairs to the breakfast lounge to talk.

"There won't be anyone in it at this time of day. Besides, my mother won't think of looking for me there."

"Won't she worry about you?"

"No, she thinks I'm with Mr. Mitchell, that he's taking me to the leather bazaar."

"And she didn't want to go along?"

"No, she said she's tired from all the walking we did this morning."

I wasn't surprised. I'd already noticed that Karen often wore skirts and high heels, as if she were attending some posh function instead of sight-seeing on foot. Even shoes with the lowest of heels were no match for the hard pavements and uneven cobblestones we constantly traveled over.

Athletic shoes might not look fashionable but were much more practical. I also thought about the fancy shoes I saw in Ferragamo's windows when we passed his building. I wondered if I could learn to walk gracefully in them.

"Doesn't your mom have any walking shoes? If not, she could probably buy some nice ones here. Why don't you suggest it?"

Kim shrugged. "She doesn't listen to me."

She took my hand and we walked past the many tables and sat on a padded bench in the corner of the breakfast room.

She frowned and looked into her lap before speaking. "I need to ask your opinion about something."

"Shoot. Just remember my opinion might not be worth much."

"Oh, I'm sure it will be. You're older, but not so old you're one of those fogeys who disapprove of anything they didn't do back in the ancient days."

I smiled. "How ancient are we talking about? Here

in Italy we've been seeing churches and buildings and statues that may be two thousand years old."

"No, not that ancient. I mean like—" She struggled for a comparison. "—like when television first started and they had sitcoms where kids were, like, totally weird."

"I've seen some of those reruns too, so I know what you mean. And, no, I wasn't even alive then." I was thinking that I sort of enjoyed reruns of those old shows. Sometimes funny is funny, even a generation later. "So what's your question?"

She looked up at me with an earnest expression. "Is it okay for a girl to have a baby if she's still in school?"

She took me totally by surprise, but I tried not to show it. "Are you thinking of doing such a thing?"

"No, not me. A couple of my friends."

I was afraid some of my shock must have filtered through anyway and made her somewhat defensive, so I kept my voice low and even. "Why do your friends want to have babies while they're so young?"

"Not all of them do, but this one girl, Tiffany, does, and she talks about it all the time."

"She's not the one you told me likes to go to Sunday school?"

"No, not that one."

I heaved a mental sigh. I'd been out of Sunday school for a long time, but I didn't think the teaching had changed *that* much.

"So, is this Tiffany sexually active?"

"She says she is, but sometimes I think she pretends." She added hurriedly, "But I know lots of girls who do it with boys."

I wanted desperately to ask Kimberly if she was having sex with boys, but I didn't. "So you want to know what I think about it, is that right?"

"Yes. You're not like my mom. We can't get good answers from our parents. They always just say 'no' to everything."

"Well, you can't blame them, can you? They're responsible for you and try to keep you safe until you're grown up."

"That's just it. They want to keep us from growing up. They try to keep us ignorant."

I patted her hand. "There's no way a parent can keep a child ignorant these days. She'd have to lock you in a closet with no radio, television, computer or telephone."

"Yeah, I guess you're right, but…"

"Okay, so here's my opinion." I felt uncomfortable being put on the spot and wanted to get the subject over with as quickly as possible. "I think having a baby at your age, or even a little older, is a huge mistake."

"How old is okay?"

"When you're out of college."

"You've got to be kidding."

"When you're married."

She really frowned that time. "People are always having babies without being married. What's the big deal about that?"

"Movie stars and other celebrities do, but, believe me, it isn't as prevalent as Hollywood and news would make you think."

"But what if you want to have a baby before you meet a guy you want to marry? Can't you have a baby anyway and then get married later?"

I could see this was going to be a lengthy session. I wished Kim would ask her mother those questions. Yet, even from what little I knew of the woman, I could understand why Kim felt she couldn't discuss them with her.

"Okay, let's look at the question from all sides. Suppose you have a baby and then later, when you meet the guy you want to marry, he says he doesn't want to raise someone else's child?"

"If he really loved me, he wouldn't say that."

I shrugged. "That's always a possibility, but I don't think it's something you can count on." I thought for a moment before I went on. "About this baby—what about the real father? Wouldn't he have something to say about raising the child?"

"Oh, boys don't want anything to do with that. They don't want to be involved and have to pay child support."

"You mean they just want to have sex with a girl and don't care what happens?"

"That's right."

"Would you want to have a baby with a boy like that for its father? I mean, the baby gets his genes too, you know. What if he's a real jerk, and your baby takes after him?"

"If he's never around, I could train the baby by myself to be a good person and not a jerk. Anyway," she added quickly, "it's not me I'm talking about. It's my friend Tiffany. I just want some advice I can give her."

"Okay, like I said, tell her she's too young."

"She's older than I am. She's almost fifteen."

"Fifteen is still too young. Her mind and body aren't fully mature, and she doesn't have the skills necessary to raise a baby. Also," and I'm afraid my voice rose a bit there, "she's too young even to *make the decision* to have a baby. We don't let fifteen-year-olds drive cars, do we?" On a roll now, I voiced all the arguments that popped into my head.

"Children shouldn't try to make adult decisions. Would a child ever go to school if it was up to him? No, he'd play video games all day."

Kim smiled at that, but I kept going.

"Do you know that, in most states a young girl who has sex, even if she wants to do it, can later charge the boy with rape, and he could go to jail? That's because the law says that fifteen-year-old girls are too young to give their consent."

Kimberly didn't answer, and I took a moment to cool down. I knew you couldn't convince someone you're right if you made them angry. I took a deep breath.

"Let's be logical." I reverted to a cool tone. "She's still in school, isn't she? Who's going to take care of that baby while she goes to classes and does homework? Who's going to babysit if she wants to go to a school football game, or a dance or on a date?"

"Her folks, I guess."

"Did she ask her folks if they want to babysit or raise another child? And pay for it, besides? Babies are very expensive, not to mention time-consuming."

"I know. You have to buy Pampers and other stuff."

"And baby food, and a crib, and a car seat, and a playpen, and things I can't even think of right now."

"She could have a baby shower and people would give her all those things."

I sighed. Those kids had answers for everything. "Well, if she's going to put the burden of that baby on other people, why does she want to have it in the first place?"

"To have someone to love, who will love her back."

"If Tiffany is never there to take care of the baby, how can she love it? And why would the baby love her? He'll grow up loving the grandparents or whoever is really taking care of him."

"You make it sound so difficult."

"Trust me, it is." I paused. "I have friends who did that very thing, and they were a whole lot older than Tiffany. They'd at least finished high school, but they didn't have parents who would take care of the baby for them. They had to go to work, and, without a college education, they couldn't get high-paying jobs. And while they were working, they had to pay a babysitter out of what little money they did earn."

Those were not mythical friends I invented to strengthen my case. Although she at least had a degree, my very own favorite college teacher had done that, and she didn't even have the pleasure of the sex. She went to a sperm bank, and now that her little boy is five and goes to kindergarten he wonders why other kids have fathers and he doesn't. However, I didn't mention sperm banks to Kim, sophisticated though she was for her age.

Kimberly looked into her lap instead of at me. I

could almost see the wheels going around in her head.

"And now," I said, "I'm going to tell you the most important reason for Tiffany not to do that." I paused like an actor trying for dramatic effect. "Because it's selfish."

I paused again to let that sink in. "She thinks she wants a baby, but what would the baby think? Would he want to be raised by a single parent, never know his real father, never have his own mother there to take care of him because she's at school or has to work, never have nice things because his mother can't afford them, never go to college either?"

"It doesn't have to be that way."

"No, it doesn't, but it probably will be. Statistics show that children raised in a home without a father are ten times more likely to use drugs or alcohol, to live in poverty, get into trouble and even end up in jail. Is that a risk Tiffany is willing to take?"

Kim didn't answer for a long time, and I felt like a fraud. I had invented that last statistic, although I'd read that the number was several times, if not exactly ten. Yet I hadn't "been there, done that" myself, so who was I to give advice?

"But so many kids I know have divorced parents, which is, well, like the same thing. And not all of them get into trouble. What about if the father dies? That can happen too, and the children turn out okay."

"That's true, but it's different. It's one thing for a child to know his parents once loved each other and wanted him, and quite another to think they didn't even care enough to get married and give him a home."

I put my arm around Kimberly's shoulders. "Look,

you don't have to tell Tiffany all of this if you don't want to. I would never have said it anyway if you hadn't asked. Plus, it's only my opinion."

She looked up at me and smiled. "I wouldn't have asked you if I didn't think you were a wise person. So thank you."

She got up from the bench, I hugged her, and we went to our respective rooms. I immediately lay down to take a nap. Acting the surrogate mother had exhausted my brain and body.

That night Enza hosted a dinner party for everyone on the tour, and afterward Taylor knocked quietly on my door and we went out into the balmy evening, walking along the Arno River and talking. Unfortunately he didn't speak about his problem, why he was a loner. He kept that to himself, as mysterious as ever.

"Have you taken lots of pictures?" I asked him. "Pictures you can turn into paintings when you get home?"

"Of course. The scenery here is incredibly beautiful."

"But you've been to Italy before. Maybe you have dozens of pictures already, just waiting to be used."

"It's true I've made several paintings from pictures I took on my previous trips, and I have a collection I can turn to when I want a new one, but I feel more inspired after being here. When I return from Rome, I can hardly wait to get out my paints and try to capture the look and the feel of the city on canvas."

"Are you a certain kind of artist, like an impressionist, or a modern or abstract painter?"

"I could never be an abstract painter. I know it's considered art, but I just can't understand it. I keep wanting to know what it's about."

I grinned, because that was another thing we had in common. "Oh, I know just what you mean. I want a picture to look like something too—a landscape, or buildings or people who look like people. All the art we've seen on this tour is so, so real."

"They call it realistic or representational art."

"So why is so-called 'modern' art so different?"

"Well, I suppose photography had something to do with that. Before photographs, the only way people could capture images was by drawing or painting them. Now, because of cameras, they don't have to."

"But who will want to see a bunch of blobs on canvas five hundred years from now? Won't they want to see what the world looked like? What our landscapes, buildings and people looked like in the twenty-first century?"

He stopped walking, and we looked down at the river for a few minutes. "You're right. A very smart woman, with an I.Q. over two hundred, said that not so long ago. Fortunately, there are a large number of artists who do exactly that kind of work."

"Good. I'd hate to think the only art available some day will be of make-believe creatures that look like they're doing something disgusting on the canvas."

He grinned again. "I promise to do my best to keep that from happening."

"So how do you paint? What's your style?"

"I'm an Impressionist. At least I try to be. I pin up my photographs and copy the image I want onto canvas as loosely as I can while still maintaining the truth of the scene."

"I wish I could see some of your paintings."

"Some day you will. I'm sure of it."

My heart did that funny loop again, and I wondered if he was serious or just another person passing through my life, hinting that we'd meet again, but knowing deep down we never would.

We walked back to the hotel hand-in-hand, and I hated to leave him and go inside my room. I felt connected to him as I never had with anyone else, and I didn't want the mood we just established to end. Yet it was almost midnight, so when he said, "Good night," I just stood very close and looked up at him. And, sure enough, he held my shoulders and kissed me properly before backing away. I really enjoyed that part of the day.

Chapter 16

Day Eight

On Thursday morning, the same tour guide took us to the famous Ufizzi Gallery where—thanks to our pre-arranged tour—we didn't have to wait in the long line outside. I loved seeing Botticelli's *Venus* and paintings by Michelangelo, Raphael and Da Vinci, but—after walking miles of corridors, climbing countless stairs and standing for ten or fifteen minutes at a time while the guide discussed, in detail, dozens of religious paintings—I began to wish I'd been allowed to wander the Gallery on my own.

More churches later, including the Basilica of San Lorenzo and the Medici chapel, Enza released us for the rest of the afternoon. Feeling as I once did at the age of ten when school was out for the summer, I almost skipped back toward the hotel. Accustomed by then to seeing Taylor with Karen or Kim—or both of them at once—during the day, I was surprised to hear his voice behind me and feel his hand on my shoulder.

"Don't scream," he whispered, "I'm kidnapping you."

I grinned, then almost ran to keep up with his long strides. He hailed a taxi, and, when one stopped in front of us, he gently but quickly pushed me inside and jumped in after me.

"To the railroad station," he told the driver, "and don't spare the horses!" Then he added something in Italian.

"Where did you get *that* expression? And why are we going to the railroad station?"

"Answer number one, in an old Western. Answer number two, we're going to Pisa. It's just an hour away by train." He looked concerned for a moment. "Is that all right?"

"Yes, I'd love to go there, but it wasn't listed on the itinerary."

"Well, this is the way to do it."

"Can we have lunch first? I'm starved."

"We'll see. First, tickets." Taylor stopped at a counter and bought tickets for us, and then he hustled me out to the platform and helped me board a train about to leave.

"Sorry, but we have no time to eat."

He was right. We barely stepped inside the coach when the train began to move. To make matters worse, so far as my stomach was concerned, there was no dining car on the train. I rummaged in my purse and managed to come up with a roll of breath mints, so we shared those and talked while the miles slipped by.

Taylor sat across from me and smiled. "I've missed you."

"What about last night?"

"That was hours ago. I want to spend all my time with you."

"I'm glad. However, I can't help noticing you aren't exactly lonely during the day."

"I feel as if I ought to be paid as a secondary tour

guide. All I do is explain what Enza and the other woman tell us, like some kind of ventriloquist. I kept wanting to tell Karen, 'Listen to them. I've never been here before. I don't know any more than you do.'" He paused. "In fact, I did say that a couple of times."

"You were being helpful and kind, as usual."

"But now I'm going to be selfish and do what I want to do, which is talk to you."

"I'm flattered. Did you enjoy the tour today?"

"Mostly."

"If it weren't for the Medicis, I think ninety percent of what we saw today would have been lost hundreds of years ago."

"I'm beginning to think my old way of going places on my own wasn't all that bad, after all. I mean, did we really need to see all forty-three monks' cells?"

His mirroring my own thoughts pleased me.

"And all that religious art. I feel as if I've seen every one of the millions of paintings from the past twenty centuries."

"I hate to agree with you on that subject, but I'm afraid I do. However, I'm trying to appreciate the fact that people in those days cared so much about Christianity they made it the focus of their lives. They erected huge churches and spent their creative talents depicting the saints in oil paints or marble."

He shrugged. "You're right, I suppose. My parents were good people, but they never went to church. My father didn't believe in organized religion. He said people could be good without going to a special building once a week."

"I think Sunday school is marvelous for children.

They learn the Ten Commandments and how to be kind to others."

"I guess that part's okay."

Being no expert, I felt out of my depth, just as I had when discussing out-of-wedlock motherhood with Kimberly. I turned my head and watched the scenery slide by outside the train windows. I admired the beautiful countryside and the many small villages we passed through.

When we arrived in Pisa, we found, much to our surprise and delight, that the railroad station contained a McDonald's restaurant. Taylor and I ordered hamburgers and chocolate milkshakes. I loved Italian food, but it was fun to have a little bit of America for a change. Especially since we could get it at all hours.

He handed me the bill. "You said you're on an expense account, so you can buy my lunch."

"*Now* you let me pay."

Afterward a taxi took us to the Leaning Tower. My first sight of the famous leaning bell tower thrilled me almost as much as being in the Colosseum. It stood, or rather leaned, stark white against a sky so blue it seemed painted there by an artist. Its decorative scrollwork gave it a look like stone lace. A wave of gratitude for the opportunity to see the magnificent structure swept over me.

However, no people waited to climb the two hundred-plus steps to the top, and we learned it was closed for minor repairs.

Taylor frowned. "I'm so sorry. I should have phoned ahead and found out. We should have come here yesterday, or tomorrow."

"But there is no tomorrow, at least not for us. We're going to Venice."

"I'm so sorry," he said again.

I touched his arm. "Don't be. It wasn't your fault. And anyway, the sun is shining today and it looks just as gorgeous as in all those pictures I've seen. Besides, I didn't particularly want to climb to the top. I'd probably faint halfway up, and you'd have to carry me down on your shoulders."

"You're just saying that to make me feel better."

I laughed and put my arm under his and led him down the path that circled the church and baptistery. Each was a beautiful building in its own right.

"Would you like to go inside?"

"No, I've been in enough big cathedrals. Let's just walk through the town."

Taylor took several pictures of the tower, most with me in the foreground, and promised to share them with me, but I insisted on getting some with my own camera. Then we strolled past stalls where vendors tried to interest us in buying souvenirs. Eventually, another taxi took us back to the railroad station and, after waiting in a long line filled mainly with noisy students carrying backpacks, we boarded the train for Florence.

As soon as we settled ourselves in the coach, Taylor leaned close to me and took my hand. "As you know, I joined this tour because of you."

"That's very flattering."

"I guess this sounds like a line or maybe a cliché, but I felt instantly attracted to you on the plane. You were so certain I was a nice person, just because I changed seats with the Frenchman. You said, 'That was very kind of you.'"

"Well, it was."

"So of course I wanted to go on talking to you." He cleared his throat. "Now I know it was right to come on this tour. What's the word for that, serendipity?"

I wasn't sure what he meant and certainly didn't want to talk about myself. "Whatever it was, I'm glad you did."

"So, now it's time for me to tell you something that's been bothering me."

"I've often felt you were hiding some secret. In fact, you said you'd tell me about it later."

"I think this is the time."

I felt my pulse race. Would I finally learn about his mysterious past?

"I told you I was trying to be less of a loner, but there's one thing I haven't mastered. I can't forgive."

Forgive? That was not what I expected him to say. Yet, relief flooded over me. He hadn't admitted he'd done some terrible thing, like my ridiculous imagination had sometimes pictured. I hadn't been wrong about his good qualities, but why would he need to forgive someone?

Chapter 17

I turned to Taylor. "Who is it you must forgive?"

"My parents."

"Your parents?" That surprised me even more.

"It's a long story, but we have an hour, and you're a captive audience." He looked away for a moment. "Unless you'd rather we talk about movies or books."

"No, I want to hear. Please tell me why you need to forgive your parents."

"I'll try to cut this down to only the essential details." He took a deep breath. "Like I said, I'm an only child. My parents were older than most when they had me, and they always regretted they never had more children."

"They say only children are spoiled, so I can imagine that they must have been doting parents."

"They were. We got along fine until the summer before I graduated from college." He rubbed his chin, as if wondering how to continue. "There was this girl, a senior in high school. She lived next door with her mother and stepfather."

A girl next door. I had said something once about it being unfortunate if we could meet only the people who lived next door, and he reacted to it with a pained expression. Apparently I had inadvertently struck a nerve.

"She was a nice girl?" I was almost afraid to ask.

"You liked her?"

"Yeah. I didn't know her all that well at first. They only moved there a year before this, er, this happened, and the family was very reclusive, stuck by themselves. My mother told me she tried to make friends with the girl's mother but nothing came of it."

"But you liked the girl?" My stomach frog had returned. I figured there was a love story in there somewhere, and I wasn't sure I wanted to hear it.

"Yes. Like I said, the family didn't make any effort to be friendly, but I saw the girl several times that summer because I worked at the supermarket, and she'd come in to buy groceries sometimes. We got to talking, and I thought she was nice."

He paused again, and I wanted to say, "Hurry up, give me the bad news, already," but I decided not to rush him.

"Being an only child, I had no one my age at home, so I always had to make friends with other kids. I guess you could say I became a little outgoing."

"You weren't a 'loner' in those days."

"Not much. So anyway, I guess I seemed, er, available to talk to, and this girl asked me to meet her on my lunch break because she wanted to ask me something in private. So, of course, I said I would. And she told me this secret."

Another long pause. I was slowly going crazy, and I wondered if it was possible to bite my fingernails down to my knuckles.

"Well, to make a long story short, she was pregnant and wanted to know if I'd help her get an abortion."

I swear my voice squeaked. "You didn't."

"No, we talked about it, and I agreed to meet her the next day. In fact, we met several times over the next two weeks, and she changed her mind about the abortion. She decided to run away instead."

"So did you help her to run away?"

"Yes. I had a little money in the bank from working every summer, and I took it out and gave it to her."

"Where did she go? Did she have plans?"

"She told me she'd leave town and change her name, so no one would know. She said she wanted to—"

"But," I interrupted, "why couldn't she tell her parents? That was how long ago? It's been fifty years since girls who got pregnant had to go away and hide."

Taylor turned sad eyes in my direction. "You don't understand. The father of the baby was... her stepfather."

I nearly fell off the train seat. "You mean he—"

"He raped her, and she was afraid to tell anyone."

"Couldn't she, at least, tell her mother?"

He lowered his head. "According to her, that was out of the question. I don't know why. I asked, but she was stubborn. Anyway, we were both young, and she had her mind made up. I just gave her the money and she went away."

"That's so sad." My thoughts swirled around the poor girl, picturing her with that terrible secret. I pictured her with Taylor, telling him, trusting him, and his helping her the best he could. After a moment, with the only sound being the train's wheels on the tracks, I remembered what had started our conversation.

"But what has that to do with you forgiving your parents?"

"Well, when the girl left town, rumors started flying. Somebody else knew, or suspected, she was pregnant, and a few people had seen us together those last few weeks so..."

"So they thought you were the father?"

"Yes. And when my parents found out I'd taken all my savings out of the bank, they put two and two together—"

"—And got five," I finished. "So why didn't you tell them the truth?"

"I'd promised I wouldn't tell anyone the full truth."

"You didn't admit to being the father of the baby, did you?"

"No, of course not. I denied it and said I didn't know who the father was. I didn't care if some people thought it was me, but my parents didn't believe me, and that hurt."

I frowned. "I'm sorry, but it sounds a bit narrow-minded of them if you ask me."

"Oh, it's not that they minded so much if I was the father. What they minded was that the girl ran away, and they blamed me for not letting them ever get to know their grandchild."

I sat back and took several deep breaths to clear my head. "They blamed you? After you'd been so kind?"

"They didn't see it that way."

I had another thought. "Wait a minute. What about a paternity test? You could have proved you weren't the father."

"Not without a baby to test, and I had no idea at the time where she'd gone."

He stood up and stretched, as if telling me the long story had given him tense muscles. Probably so. Mine were so tense I felt like a tree stump.

"So they never forgave you for this misunderstanding?"

"And I never forgave them either. I felt they should have believed me, even without a paternity test."

"So?"

"So, I left home and I've never been back." He sat down again. "We don't communicate with one another."

I felt chilled by his words but couldn't think of anything to say.

"I'm sorry," he said abruptly. "Maybe it was wrong to tell you, to air my family's dirty laundry."

"Not at all, but, I mean, are you sure you didn't misinterpret their feelings? Maybe if you had just talked to your mom and dad about it."

"I was so hurt that they believed the rumors instead of me. I felt if they wouldn't believe me, they never really loved me."

My voice was firm. "Of course they loved you."

At another level, I knew some parents did not love their own children. Child abuse cases often made newspaper headlines. Yet I remained convinced that most people did, my own family and that of all my friends being the norm. On the other hand, there was this girl's mother who allowed her own husband to...but probably she didn't know about it. Probably the girl thought she wouldn't be believed if she told her mother.

"No," Taylor was saying, "my parents couldn't have loved me or they wouldn't have been like that. At least they seemed that way at the time. I'm afraid I said some really terrible things to them." He rubbed his hand across his forehead as if wanting to rub out the memory of the hateful remarks. "Look, I probably shouldn't have dumped this on you. I'm sorry."

"It's all right. I'm not upset. In fact, I'm flattered you can confide in me. I wish I could help."

"You have helped already. Right from the first." He took my hand again and looked deeply into my eyes. "Everything about you seemed to tell me you'd understand."

"I'm sure trying."

"Look at how you've been on this tour. You put up with Karen's behavior, never saying anything bad about her, even when other people did."

Except my thoughts were often unkind. I tried to remember if I'd ever voiced any of those aloud.

"And you took so much time with Kim and showed such patience and understanding."

He didn't even know about the long talk I'd had with the girl. What if I'd said all the wrong things to her? A great writer once said, "Wisdom comes to us when it can no longer do any good." I felt utterly incompetent at that moment, but Taylor needed my words then, right or not. I swallowed.

"I think by now you've already realized that was only a misunderstanding, and it should have been cleared up a long time ago."

"I know. I tell myself I should go and see them,

and we'll just laugh at the past. Yet, somehow I keep putting it off. I know I can't put it off forever. They're older, and I don't want them to die before we resolve this. Meanwhile, I can't seem to make the hurt go away."

"I'm no counselor, but I think you need to forgive them."

"I know that, and I sometimes tell myself that if I do, it will all be over."

"I'm sure it would be."

"Maybe, maybe not. Nevertheless, I guess I shouldn't have told you all my troubles."

"I'm glad you did. We've become— well, good friends on this tour. Besides, sometimes talking helps."

"Talking to you helps, anyway. I know that." He brought my hand to his lips.

The train came to a stop in Florence and we walked back to the hotel from the station, Taylor keeping a firm grip on my hand. He found a pizza shop, and we ate our impromptu dinner on the darkened patio beside it, sitting close on the narrow bench so I felt his arms and thighs brushing against mine. As we left, some shops were closing, and he gently pulled me into a darkened doorway, put his arms around me and kissed me.

His kisses were everything I imagined they would be, his lips firm but tender. I let my arms find their way to his back, pressed tightly and returned the pressure of his kiss. How right it felt. I wanted to stay in his arms forever. I needed Taylor's warmth and comfort as much as he needed mine. And, although I didn't know how, I wanted to help him find a way to resolve his estrangement from his parents.

After a long moment, we broke apart and walked to the hotel. We stepped into the lighted lobby and took the lift to my floor. After unlocking my door, he took me in his arms and we kissed again. "Good night," he whispered, his voice husky.

I closed the door and leaned back against it, remembering everything we said and did that day. I still felt the taste of his mouth, the warm smoothness of his neck under my fingers, the touch of his cheek on mine. The frog in my middle had turned into something more like a rapidly beating heart. Perhaps I was really in love.

Chapter 18

Day Nine

The next morning, Taylor sat next to me in the van on the way to Venice, apparently deciding to make no effort to pretend we were not a couple. I both enjoyed and worried about it. I could almost feel Karen Vale throw icy darts at my back.

In Venice, our van parked, and we transferred to a water taxi to go to our hotel. Although the hotel itself fronted on a wide canal, the taxi driver steered his boat into a narrow waterway on the side. A small dock bobbed on the water, and men in uniforms helped us up a few steps to the lobby. Our luggage was marked in chalk with our room numbers and delivered to us later.

My room was luxurious and held a king-sized bed, with two overstuffed chairs and a table at its foot, plus a good-sized chest of drawers for clothes. My large window faced a side garden which, although a floor below me, was so lovely I took a picture of it. Inside the closet, a small safe had been provided where I could store money and travelers checks if I preferred not to carry them with me. I made use of those safes in every hotel we stayed in, taking only a small amount of cash in a tiny purse when I went out.

The bathroom was especially large, with separate areas for everything. One side contained a huge glass-enclosed shower stall which looked inviting as well as glamorous. So inviting, in fact, that I decided to use it right away. However, when I stepped inside and turned the knob, the showerhead threw water everywhere, drenching everything in sight, not to mention my hair and the towel I had expected to use to dry myself.

A little later, still feeling slightly damp, I met the rest of the group in the seating area of the lobby, and Enza introduced us to Maria, who took us on a tour of, guess what, churches. Maria boasted that hers was about "hidden Venice," not the usual tour of the city, but while walking along the Grand Canal and its little cousins, we saw the famous Piazza San Marco, and both the Rialto Bridge and the Bridge of Sighs. We went inside St. Mark's cathedral, a couple of other churches, and of course, saw the Doges' Palace.

Kimberly chased pigeons and scrambled up and down bridges, and I marveled at how one moment she acted like a child, whereas on the previous day she'd been discussing sex and babies.

That night Taylor and I had dinner in the hotel's outdoor restaurant, which was almost under my room window. It was secluded on two sides by white stucco walls covered in vines and on the others by large leafy trees, shrubs and flowers. A small group of musicians played appropriate dinner music, and the food, served buffet style, was excellent.

Afterward we walked along the plaza and over a bridge or two, but didn't go very far.

"I've been to Venice before," Taylor said, "but it's easy to get lost here."

"You," I joked, "with a GPS in your head?"

"I try to stay close to the Grand Canal and the big hotels. The narrow streets can be confusing."

"It's so strange not to see cars, only sidewalks, bridges and water."

"That's what makes Venice unique of all the cities in the world. Unfortunately, it floods at times. I just hope we don't lose the city entirely one day."

I'd seen a documentary on television about one of the plans to save the city through the use of gates that would rise up out of the bay, and I mentioned it to Taylor.

"They hit upon that idea at least ten years ago, but it never happens. No politician actually wants to take the responsibility of starting such an expensive project." He shook his head. "It's really amazing. As brilliant as the Italians are, they can't seem to get their act together. I mean, good grief, the Dutch saved Amsterdam from the sea."

"Get a Dutchman to run for mayor." I meant it as a joke, of course, but the thought of Venice sinking forever into the sea depressed me, and I was glad when Taylor changed the subject.

We walked for several minutes in a comfortable silence until Taylor said, "I want you to know how much I've loved being on this tour with you. I wish it didn't have to end."

I felt that frog croak in my middle again. Taylor was talking as if our relationship was doomed to end, as if he hadn't kissed me so often lately. As if he didn't intend to ever see me again. While all the time I'd been thinking something entirely different.

Men looked at love, romance and sex from a

different perspective. Perhaps, to him, this was just a nice vacation, including a few passionate kisses with a female tourist to make it more interesting.

So I didn't voice what I felt, because it was beginning to look as if he didn't have similar feelings. I tried to sound nonchalant. "We have two more days here in Venice."

"But then you'll go back to California."

"And you'll go on to Lake Como."

"Come with me. It's beautiful, and you'll love it."

Well, at least he asked me to go there with him. That was something, even though we both knew I couldn't. "I can't. My boss expects me back, and I have to write up my article for the next issue of the magazine."

"I'd love to show you the lake and the dozens of little villages around it, and the supermarket."

"You want to show me a supermarket?" The tension I'd been feeling broke at that, and I laughed. "We have those in California. In fact, unless I'm very much mistaken, we probably invented the concept."

"Oh, Americans think they invented everything. Being in Italy should have cured you of that by now." He hurried on. "Anyway, you've never seen a supermarket like this before. It's called Bennett's."

"A grand old Italian name," I joked, but I remembered seeing signs that read "Bennett's" as we traveled to Venice in the van.

"No, really. This is not like any other supermarket. It's so huge, even the word 'super' doesn't do it justice."

"Bigger than Costco?"

"Multiply that by ten."

"You're not serious."

"They bring in food from all over the world—entire aisles with nothing but varieties of apples, aisles of different pears, long aisles of cheese, aisles of pasta."

"Enough already. I get the picture."

"So you'll come with me and I'll take you there?"

"So I will *not* come with you. Maybe I'll see it some other time."

He shrugged. "Party pooper."

I grinned. "If we were at the Trevi Fountain now, I could throw in a coin and wish to go to Lake Como some day."

Taylor reached in his pocket and pulled out a handful of coins. "Quick, make a wish." At that, he threw the coins into the canal.

"It's a deal." I grinned.

He drew me into his arms and we kissed. Just as before, my lips clung to his, my arms encircled him as his did me, and I could feel his heart beat beneath his fancy new Italian shirt. When we broke apart, he smiled as if he'd enjoyed it but said nothing. I tried to pretend I didn't feel anything more than he apparently did.

We kissed again just outside the hotel lobby, and again in the elevator and at my doorway. We lingered together in the semi-dark hallway, holding each other close. I knew then what it felt like to want the moment to go on and on and never end. I wanted us to go through the open door into my bedroom and make love. I wanted to feel every inch of his firm body next to mine. I wanted his mouth on my skin, leaving kisses on my bare flesh.

Then I asked myself why. I'd had plenty of

opportunities to say "yes" and start an affair with someone, but I never wanted to until now. I always wanted a commitment first, Why this man and this particular time? Was it being so far away from home? Was it the spell of Venice? I couldn't answer that. Somehow making love with him just seemed so right.

He whispered in my ear, his voice soft but trembling slightly. "Sydney. My darling Sydney, I have no right to ask you..."

"Don't ask," I whispered back. "I don't want to say 'no.'"

He kissed me feverishly again, his own desire evident in the pressure of his hands caressing my back and hips.

"Sydney!"

It was not Taylor's voice that made me back away and the two of us break apart as if we were illicit lovers caught by a previously unsuspecting spouse. It was Kimberly.

Wearing a long nightgown, her hair loose and flowing around her face, she screamed my name again and ran to me. Taylor pulled away barely in time for her to clasp me around the middle and bury her wet, sobbing face in my chest. "Sydney, save me!"

I had just enough presence of mind to grasp the situation and put my arms around her. "Kimberly, what's the matter? What happened?"

Her words came in short gasps. "A vampire chased me! He wants to kill me!"

I spoke in as soothing a tone as I could manage under the circumstances. "There are no vampires here. We're in a hotel in Venice and you only had a bad dream."

She managed to raise her head and look at me, as if suddenly aware of her surroundings. "In a hotel? But I saw him. I know I did."

"You had a bad nightmare. You've been reading another vampire novel, haven't you?"

She pulled away and rubbed a hand over her eyes. "I thought, I mean..."

"It's all over now. You're awake and there's no vampire chasing you. Wash your face, get a drink of water and go back to bed." I glanced toward Taylor, who had retreated to a dark corner of the hall, his face a faint gray in the shadows.

"No." Kim ran into my bedroom and jumped onto the bed. "I'm too scared."

"Go to your mother. She'll comfort you."

"She's not in our room. I don't know where she is."

I spoke from the doorway. "Go back to your room anyway. When she returns she'll be worried if you're not there."

"She won't even know. We have twin beds and she's... she's... you have a big bed. I can sleep with you, can't I? Then I know I'll be safe."

I glanced toward Taylor again, only he was no longer in the hallway. Evidently he already guessed what would follow. I closed the door and changed into my nightgown. Before I finished removing my makeup and brushing my teeth, Kim was asleep.

I crawled into bed beside her where I planned to pick up the thread of my expected romantic moment in my own dreams. I comforted myself by remembering that, as I'd said to Taylor, we did have two more days.

Perhaps, sometime during those days, we could continue down the romantic road we'd almost begun to travel. Not only that, perhaps Taylor would say he loved me too. Perhaps, he'd even say something about our future.

Chapter 19

Day Ten

When I awoke the next morning, Kim was already gone, so I showered—this time with the towel *outside* the enclosure—dressed and went down to breakfast. The entire tour group met again in the lobby where Enza told the rest of us that Karen wasn't feeling well. She asked us to wait half an hour, while she went with Kimberly to their assigned room.

She returned with the girl. "I'm afraid Mrs. Vale will not be joining us this morning."

"Still sick?" John Parker asked. "I remember when I talked to her yesterday she complained about not feeling well. Should she see a doctor?"

"She does not seem to have a fever, only nausea, and she thinks the boat trip to the other islands might make it worse." She shrugged. "But I will look in on her when we return, and I will call a doctor if necessary."

Kimberly, released from her mother's attention, grabbed Taylor's hand. "You'll be my guide today, won't you?"

He smiled down at her and assured her he would.

I immediately felt guilty. I admitted to myself that I didn't like Karen, but knew I ought to change my attitude. True, she hadn't been in her room the night before when Kim needed her—and I didn't—but I hoped she wasn't seriously ill and would soon be well. I also vowed that the next time I saw Karen, I'd make it a point to be pleasant and kind.

Taylor managed to say a few quiet words to me that the others couldn't hear, and I took it to mean he too wanted to repeat the events of the night before, only with a different, more satisfying, ending.

We boarded the same water taxi that brought us to the hotel the day before. The small craft waited at the dock, and Enza told us she had engaged it for the day. We sped off immediately toward several other islands. Enza had told us on the van ride that, although Venice consisted of over a hundred islands—all joined by bridges–the larger islands, farther east in the bay, contained interesting sights as well.

Our first stop was at Murano with its world-renowned glass-making factories. Enza said the factories were once located in Venice but were moved to the other island because of danger from the fires they required. As we watched, I thrilled at the sight of the glass blower's skill.

Suddenly aware Kimberly was no longer at my side, I looked around, but didn't see the girl anywhere.

"She's probably in one of the other display rooms," Taylor said. "There are so many, I'm almost feeling lost myself."

Fifteen minutes later, I spotted her talking to a girl about her own age at the sales counter. When she saw Taylor and me, she rushed over. "This is Amy and her brother Paul. They're staying in the hotel right next to ours."

Amy, who looked about thirteen, and Paul, perhaps

fifteen, were attractive young Americans. Their parents were completing the purchase of a green glass tree branch that sported five exotic colored glass birds.

After introducing us to the Cartwrights, her new friends' family, Kimberly bought a souvenir—a small blue and white fish—with her own money. "It's a bargain. Only fourteen American dollars."

That accomplished, we walked back down to the dock, and the water taxi took us to Burano, another island built on canals. Much to Kim's delight, the Cartwright family showed up there as well. She skipped through the town with Amy and Paul, darting in and out of shops and generally behaving like a teenager on a lark.

Burano was known for its lace-making, so I asked Taylor to keep an eye on the young people while I looked over what the shops had to offer. Besides blouses, dresses and scarves, they sold exquisite table linens, and I imagined the day when I'd have a house of my own, with a real dining room set on which I'd place a genuine Italian lace tablecloth. I dream expensive.

Half an hour later, I strolled the street and found Taylor, his camera up to his eyes, taking pictures.

"Do you think you'll paint any of this?"

"Wouldn't you?" He lowered the camera. "I'm indebted to you again. If it hadn't been for this tour, I might never have come to this island."

"I suspect it would only be a matter of time."

Kimberly came running up. "Isn't it beautiful? There aren't any cars, only boats, just like Venice. And there's even a small leaning tower." She grinned, then turned and ran off again to catch up with Amy and Paul.

The Cartwrights joined us for lunch on the outdoor patio at Romano's, a restaurant whose menu recounted the many political figures, movie stars, and other celebrities who had dined there. Then Taylor, Kim and I walked back to our water taxi.

The next island was Torchello, now almost a ghost town, with only two remaining churches in the midst of grass and weeds. The few inhabitants also sold lace and little shops offered souvenirs.

After touring the finest of the churches, we found Kimberly sitting on a large stone that somewhat resembled a giant chair. "Look," she called, "it's the Chair of Attila. Quick, take my picture sitting in it."

She struck a pose probably intended to be queen-like and Taylor snapped her picture with both hers and his own cameras.

"There's room for more than one," Kim said. "Come sit with me. Both of you."

So Taylor called to Lance to take a picture of the three of us crowded into the stone seat. He obligingly took several, and then Taylor reciprocated by taking some of Lance and Robin, hugging of course, and even one with Robin perched on Lance's lap. We all giggled at the results.

When it was time to return to Venice, Kim and I sat outside the water taxi's cabin, letting the breeze ruffle our hair and talking to the driver. I thought I had never seen the girl so animated. What a difference from her demeanor when her mother was around.

Our craft slowed down when it entered the Grand Canal and then slowed even further to negotiate the turn into the narrow canal which led to our hotel entrance. I was watching the scenery when suddenly I heard shouts. I turned around and saw Kimberly standing up.

The captain—or whatever they call water-taxi drivers— along with Taylor and Lance Waxman, was yelling at her to sit down, that it was dangerous to stand up while we were still moving. Then I saw Kim lean forward, and I had a sudden, sick feeling she was going to fall overboard. I just reacted. I was closest to her and I knew I had to keep her from falling into the canal.

At the last second I heard her shout, "My fish!" and she was apparently not in danger of going overboard herself, but had dropped her new souvenir. But it was too late.

This all happened in an instant and, thanks to three men's arms grabbing for me, I was hauled back into the boat almost immediately. To be sure, I was wet and embarrassed as I'd never been before. I wished I could hide under the wooden seat and die like a hooked tarpon.

But the good news was that, thanks to my going overboard, the glass fish got caught in my sweater where I had tied the sleeves in a knot at my waist, and we were both pulled to safety.

The driver steered us to the dock, and an ever-present doorman tied up the craft. As he helped me out, he gave me an open-mouthed stare, and I squished up the steps and into the lobby with his voice saying, "Americani!" echoing in my head.

However, Kim was grateful I had saved her fish from a watery grave—after all, he wasn't the kind with real fins—and kept apologizing for my accident. I assured her no harm was done and hurried to my room where I stripped, took another shower and dressed in dry clothes.

Taylor hadn't suggested we meet that afternoon, and I debated taking a nap. However, I wanted to see more of Venice, so I returned to the plaza in front of the hotel. I spent almost an hour wandering among the many booths where vendors sold hats, scarves, postcards and a great many original oil paintings.

Finally Taylor appeared at my side. "I think I need to kidnap you again. I want to ride in a gondola, and I can't very well do it without you."

I smiled at him. "What about the others?" I teased. "Don't they want to go too?"

"If so, they'll just have to do it without us. I want to be like James Bond in that old film, *From Russia With Love*. Remember that?"

I pretended to be annoyed. "The movies have a lot to answer for. Well, all right, I'm game." Then I had a sudden thought. "What about Kimberly? Is her mother okay? Are we supposed to be looking out for her?"

"She's doing her own sightseeing with the Cartwrights."

"Is that all right with Karen?"

"We didn't ask, but the Cartwrights seem to be a nice family. And besides, we checked it out with Enza. She should be the one playing 'mother-hen,' not you."

I shrugged. "Well, I suppose it's normal for Kim to want to be with another girl her age."

"Frankly, I think it's Paul who interests her most." Taylor pulled me along toward the row of waiting gondolas.

I remembered our conversation of the day before and hoped that Paul's parents were acting as chaperones for the young people. Still, as Taylor had reminded me, that was not my problem. Some day I hoped to have children of my own, and then I could let myself get paranoid over their whereabouts.

We'd reached the dock, and Taylor helped me into the rocking vessel, seating me in the well-padded stern. He dropped down next to me, and the boatman, wearing the traditional striped shirt and straw hat with a ribbon, skillfully maneuvered the gondola into the canal.

Taylor pulled out his camera and focused it on the many picturesque houses that lined the canals as well as the ornate bridges over the water. Every turn brought new vistas that screamed to be reproduced on film or canvas.

Finally Taylor stopped taking pictures, sat back and put his arm around me. "I can't let this romantic moment get away." He leaned over and kissed me.

I felt, indeed, like an actress in a Hollywood film. Even if I never saw Taylor again, I would always cherish the memory of sailing with a handsome man in a gondola in Venice.

When Taylor broke the kiss, I said, "Can't you get the gondolier to sing a romantic Italian song?"

"That would make the moment complete, wouldn't it?" He put his other arm around me and pulled me close. "But we'll just have to settle for this." Once more I felt his lips on mine.

A minute later he said, "Would you be upset if I told you I think I'm falling in love with you?"

I remembered the night before, and my heart began to swell. "Not on your life."

"I know we've known each other—" He stopped to do a mental count. "–Eleven days, but I'm sure even tonight won't be the end for us."

I only said, "Tonight?" as if I didn't know what was coming, and he kissed me again. I'd never been so happy.

* * *

Back in my room, I changed clothes, and at seven thirty I followed Enza and the others down narrow streets and up and down at least eight bridges, to the appointed restaurant for dinner. As we walked, Kimberly held tightly to Taylor's hand. Enza reported that Karen, although feeling better, did not want to come to dinner with us.

That time I sat next to Taylor, and, instead of sitting on his other side, Kimberly took a chair across the long table from us, as if wanting to establish her independence. She struck what she might have decided was a haughty pose and ordered her own dinner from the menu.

We finished our meal and were waiting for dessert when Karen showed up. She wore a raincoat against the sudden shower out of doors, and her hair—normally always in place—looked disheveled. Her face bore a scowl, mouth curved downward, eyes narrowed into menacing slits. At the sight of her, all conversation stopped, and everyone stared in her direction.

I felt my stomach muscles constrict, as if they sensed

something bad was about to happen. I wondered if Karen had found out about Kimberly spending time with the Cartwright family and disapproved. Would she yank the girl from her seat and drag her back to the hotel? But the reality was much worse.

"I want you all to know," Karen said in a voice loud enough to attract diners at other tables, "that something terrible has been going on." She paused dramatically, as if making sure she had everyone's attention.

"Mr. Taylor Mitchell—" She paused. "—has sexually molested my daughter."

Chapter 20

Tears blurred my vision, my heart felt as if it had stopped beating, and my breath caught. This was unreal, impossible. In the silence that seemed to go on forever, I stared at Karen, and then looked down at Kimberly. The girl seemed traumatized by the accusation, her face drained of all color, her eyes and mouth open wide. I wondered if she tried to scream, but no sound came forth.

Enza jumped to her feet. At the same time, Kimberly, as if emerging from a trance, shouted, "No! No!" lowered her head and pounded her fists on the table.

Still in shock, I realized Taylor, next to me, was standing, and I turned to look at him. His fists were clenched at his sides, his face a tight, pale mask, lips thinned, and eyes narrowed. I stood too and reached out to touch him, but before I could say a word, he backed up so violently he sent his chair crashing backward onto the floor and stalked from the restaurant.

Enza strode toward Karen, her voice low, almost menacing. "You will please take your daughter back to the hotel. This is not the place. This is not the time." When no one moved, she added, in a stern tone that I'd never heard her use before, "Do as I say."

I found my own voice at last. "It's not true."

Enza glanced at me, and then looked at everyone

around the table. "Do not speak of this. I will handle the problem." She gently pulled Kimberly from her seat and walked her to the door. Karen, head erect, glaring as if defying anyone to say a word, followed them out.

My knees wobbly, my head spinning, I slumped back in the chair. As if in a dream, I heard the murmuring of others at the table as well as in the rest of the restaurant's main dining room.

"It's not true," I said again, but—when Robin Waxman looked at me as if waiting for an explanation—I didn't know what to say. I felt certain Taylor was an honorable man. Furthermore he could not have been so attentive to me, kissing me, telling me he was in love with me, and still abuse a little girl.

Yet, where was the proof? I had not been with Taylor every moment of every day. Just that afternoon, I had been walking on the piazza alone for some time before he took me for the gondola ride. Afterward, we had gone to our separate rooms to change clothes. In truth, I didn't know what he'd been doing during those times.

My heart pounded in my chest, and my throat became dry as dust. "I don't care," I said at last. "I know it. I just know it. It's a lie. He did not abuse Kimberly." I got to my feet again, grabbed my purse and jacket from the chair, and stumbled to the doorway. I opened it and strode outside.

I saw no one. Not Enza. Not Karen, Kimberly, or Taylor. I felt heavy raindrops on my head but ignored them. I searched in vain for a glimpse of Taylor, but finally went back inside the restaurant. I would have walked all the way to the hotel myself, rain or not, but

I didn't know the way. I could never remember which narrow streets Enza guided us into, or what bridges we'd crossed.

I spoke to the others at the table. "How do we get back to the hotel? Does anyone know the way?"

Heads shook in denial. Lance Waxman said, "I might be able to do it, but I think it's best if we take a water taxi. I'll ask the head waiter to order it for us." He rose, disappeared for a moment and returned to say that water taxis were busy because of the rain. He said it would be at least twenty minutes before we could get one.

I went into the ladies' restroom and closed myself into a stall where I could cry without being seen. My shoulders shook, great sobs wracked my body, and my eyes burned with overflowing tears. For Taylor. That anyone should accuse him of such a terrible thing made me want to scream and tear things. I hadn't felt so frustrated, angry and impotent since being told of my brother Howard's death. Why did bad things happen to good people? Why?

* * *

Eventually, the water taxi arrived and took us back to the hotel. I rushed to Taylor's room and knocked on the door. No answer. I knocked again. Still no answer. Then it occurred to me he might not want to see any of the others.

I spoke loudly. "Taylor, it's me, Sydney. Please open the door."

Again no answer, not even, "Go away."

So he didn't want to talk about it. I could understand that. Maybe he wasn't even in his room. Perhaps he was still outdoors, walking the streets, or in a bar getting drunk. I was sure that, under the circumstances, some men might do that very thing. At the least, he was probably in shock too. Unless, of course, he was guilty, but I didn't believe that.

I finally gave up and went to my own room, undressed and crawled into bed, but sleep failed to arrive. Over and over in my mind, the awful scene replayed itself. Karen making her dreadful announcement, Kimberly looking devastated, Taylor bolting from the restaurant. And I—what had I done? Only stared in disbelief, and then finally protested it was a lie. Did anyone believe me? Did I believe it myself?

The doubts I'd had at the table returned. I didn't know where Taylor had been at certain hours. For that matter, there were plenty of times during the tour that I hadn't seen him at all. He could have been anywhere, doing anything.

I tossed in bed, stomach churning. What if he *had* abused Kimberly? I remembered the way he left the restaurant, not saying anything, not denying the charge. That alone must make him look guilty.

I also remembered Kimberly's reaction to her mother's statement. First, open-mouthed amazement. Then that cry, "No!" and beating her fists on the table. What did that mean? Was it embarrassment? Was she denying Taylor had touched her or upset because her mother accused him in front of everyone?

I turned in the bed again, the bedclothes tangling around my legs. I felt confused and angry, but mainly I felt helpless. I didn't know what to do, or if I could do anything. In spite of my strong feelings for Taylor, I felt as if I were a bystander in a tragic drama. And yet, I knew my doubts were unfounded. I knew Taylor was innocent. Eventually I slept.

* * *

Day Eleven

In the morning, I again tried Taylor's door, but when he didn't answer, I wondered if he'd gone downstairs for breakfast. Oh, get real, I told myself. He's just been accused of child molestation, and he's going to calmly eat eggs and toast? Even though I wasn't cold, I shivered.

I entered the large dining room anyway, because that's where everyone had been meeting every morning, and I didn't know what else to do. Sure, I could go out now that it was daylight and the rain had stopped and try to find Taylor. But even if I could keep from getting lost—and, with a stab of pain, I remembered how Taylor had pointed out signs that directed tourists toward the Grand Canal—I felt it would be hopeless. Besides, someone, probably Enza, would know where he was.

Inside the large, cheerful room, buffet tables offering what now seemed normal, greeted me. I saw a few other hotel guests serving themselves from the platters, but no one else from my tour. After hesitating a few moments, I picked up a plate and approached the many food dishes, but became queasy and couldn't imagine eating anything. I made a cup of tea and took it to a table in the corner to wait for the others.

A few minutes later, Mary and John Parker joined me. John went to the buffet table to get his breakfast, but Mary sat down next to me and spoke softly, kindly.

"I can imagine how you must feel, and I want you to know that both John and I believe Taylor is innocent."

I mumbled a "thank you."

"We've lived longer than you, and we've interacted with many, many people. I don't think we could have been that wrong about Taylor Mitchell. I simply can't believe he would ever do such a terrible thing."

I remembered my doubts from the night before. "We've only known him for a few days. Isn't it possible?"

"Anything is possible, but in Taylor's case, I find it highly *improbable* that he's such a monster and we wouldn't suspect."

"I hope and pray you're right."

John returned with a filled plate. "You hope what's right?"

"She hopes I'm right to say Taylor is innocent of Karen's accusation." Mary stood up and headed for the buffet table, and John sat down on my other side.

"That Karen." He shook his head. "She's a piece of work. I've met women like her before. A predator, out for something, and when she doesn't get it, she has to spoil life for everybody else."

"Out for— you mean Taylor."

"For Taylor, of course. It's been obvious right from the start that she set her cap for him." He paused.

"Excuse me for using such an old-fashioned expression, but that's what we would have called it in my day."

Robin and Lance Waxman entered the dining room and came toward us. While John and Lance brought more chairs, Robin headed for the buffet and returned soon with a glass of orange juice.

As Lance went to get his own food, Robin leaned toward me. "Don't be upset. We're on your side."

I tried to smile. "You think Taylor is innocent?"

Robin didn't answer for a moment and just sipped her juice. "Well, of course, we don't know him all that well, but you spent time with him. If you're certain, then we are too."

Her comment didn't reassure me very much, and I put my cup to my lips to hide my trembling mouth. I didn't want to cry again, not in public. "But where is he? Has anyone seen him since last night?"

Robin shook her head, and the others looked equally perplexed.

Lance returned and sat down. "Great food, isn't it?"

"Oh, Lance." Robin sounded impatient. "How can anyone eat this morning?"

"I can. I don't have a guilty conscience."

"Lance!"

His face flushed, and he looked at me. "Sorry. That just sort of slipped out. I mean, we don't think Taylor really— that is—"

"What Lance is trying to say," Robin offered, "is that it might not have been his fault."

"What do you mean?" Mary Parker asked.

"Well, let's be realistic. Kimberly is thirteen and nowadays girls are very sophisticated."

"Some girls, even in my office," Lance said, "dress and act like hookers."

"And," Robin went on, "you have to admit that she hung around him a lot. It's obvious she had a crush on him."

"No," I said, "it wasn't like that. She treated him more like a father. She looked up to him."

"Well, I could be wrong," Robin said, "but *if* Kimberly was flattered by his attention, and *if* Taylor was the kind of man who would take advantage of that—well, I'm just saying, it might have happened."

I listened but couldn't believe Robin's theory. I knew that never happened. Then, my conversation with Kimberly about teenagers having babies leaped into my mind. Did Kimberly want to get pregnant? No, I told myself, that wasn't Kimberly, that was her friend. Right, I also told myself, like people never pretend it's someone else they're talking about. Was it possible Robin was right, and Kimberly had such a crush on Taylor that she'd seduce him? I couldn't make myself believe she thought of him as anything but a father figure.

I'd awakened that morning with a firm conviction justice would be done, and nothing anyone said would convince me otherwise. My voice rose. "I won't believe that. Taylor did not do anything to Kimberly and I don't believe she wanted him to."

Mary touched my hand. "I agree with you, and I applaud you for having faith in him."

"I hope you're right," Robin said. "I really do."

"Me, too," Lance said. He added, "Oh-oh, look who's coming." He jumped up and pulled over another small table and then I saw Enza and Kimberly.

John also got up and the men brought over more chairs. Enza, her arm around Kimberly's shoulder, led the girl to the expanded table and they sat. No one spoke for a long moment.

Enza looked around at the group. "I am happy to say that the, er, problem is over. I assure you the thing Mrs. Vale said—it was not true."

Kimberly, eyes red from crying, spoke in a shaky voice. "I don't know why my mother said what she did. It isn't true and she knows it."

"But why?" John Parker asked.

"She thought— I don't know."

Enza spoke again. "For most of the day yesterday, Kimberly was with a nice American family, the Cartwrights, and Mrs. Vale leaped to a wrong conclusion. She is sorry now. I spoke to her a few minutes ago, and she has asked me to apologize to all of you."

Mary Parker asked, "But why would she make such an accusation?"

"She took medication for her sickness," Enza said, "and she thinks it made her... I'm afraid I do not know the English word."

"Paranoid?" Robin said.

While others murmured their own version, Lance muttered, "Probably sloshed as well."

Remembering Karen's indulgence in plenty of wine at dinner and Kimberly having told me her mother often drank liquor at home, I thought Lance might be closer to the truth. Furthermore, where was she the night before when Kim had her nightmare about a vampire? The excuse that her medication made her do it sounded almost as lame as the customary, "My dog ate my homework."

Gradually, their appetites apparently restored, Robin and Lance returned to the buffet.

I remained at the table with Kimberly. I put my arm around the girl, and she clutched my hand and looked up at me. "Mr. Mitchell never—" She didn't finish and didn't need to.

"I know." I turned to Enza. "Do you believe what Karen said?"

Enza asked Kimberly to please bring her a plate of fruit, and when the girl was safely out of earshot, she turned to me and spoke softly. "When we returned from the restaurant, I told Mrs. Vale she had made a serious charge, and I would have to call the police and they would make a report." She glanced up before continuing. "Then Mrs. Vale admitted she had spoken wrongly, that, because of her sickness and the medicine, she wasn't herself."

"And what about Mr. Mitchell?" I said. "Did Mrs. Vale apologize to him? Has anyone told him she admitted it was a lie?"

Enza shook her head slowly. "No. I am sorry. The desk clerk has told me that late last night Mr. Mitchell has checked out of the hotel."

Karen's words the night before had been bad enough. Then, the news that Taylor had gone tightened my throat and turned my body cold. The day before, I'd been beginning to feel that I was falling in love with him. That Mr. Right had shown up to prove anything was possible. But then Karen had made her accusation, and now that my faith in him had just been restored, he was gone. I'd never see him again, and he'd never know Karen had admitted she lied.

Chapter 21

After breakfast I went to my room and fell across the bed. I was grateful the truth had been revealed, but what should I do now? Continuing the tour seemed unnatural, unreal. Maybe Enza was downstairs even then, organizing something with the others, but I couldn't bring myself to be a part of it. How could I go sightseeing and pretend to enjoy myself when my mind was stuck in shock and concern?

Yet what else could I do? I had one more day on my schedule, a day I was supposed to be gathering information for my article. Actually, I didn't need more knowledge. I already had enough for twenty articles, to say nothing of the facts in the guidebooks.

Should I go home a day early? That held no more appeal than staying in Venice.

Wait, there was something. After learning Taylor had checked out of the hotel, I doubted I would ever see him again, but then I remembered he told me he was going to Lake Como and even mentioned the name of the hotel. A sudden impetuosity, which was not unusual in my case, overcame me, and I knew I had to leave Venice right away and go to Lake Como. I had to find Taylor and tell him what happened after he left. I jumped off the bed and packed my clothes.

Half an hour later, downstairs in the lobby, I decided to leave a message for Enza, and I hurried to one of the little desks in a corner. As I expected, I found the hotel kept some stationery there for that very purpose. When I finished writing the note, I spied Kimberly sitting on one of the sofas looking morose.

I walked over to her. "Are you okay?"

"Yeah, I guess."

"Don't be too hard on your mother. I'm sure she feels just as bad about this misunderstanding as the rest of us."

"But she'll never admit it."

"If she needs help—" I started.

"She never listens to me."

"Maybe she'd listen to someone else."

"Like who?"

"A school counselor?"

She groaned. "I couldn't do that."

"There must be someone." I sat down next to her. "What about her boss? Didn't you tell me she works for a plastic surgeon? Well, in that case, he's a doctor."

"So?"

"So doctors know other kinds of doctors, and besides they keep things confidential. Maybe you could find a time to talk to him and ask him to recommend someone who could help your mother."

"Maybe." Nevertheless, she didn't look all that enthusiastic about the prospect.

I filled in the silence that followed. "Did your mother know you were with the Cartwrights and not Mr. Mitchell yesterday?"

"I told her."

"Did you and Paul—?" I didn't finish. I hated even to think what I was thinking.

"No, of course not. We didn't do anything. Besides, Amy was there too." She paused and spoke softly. "Not that I wouldn't like to. I'd do anything to get away from my mom."

Our conversation about teenagers having babies flashed across my mind again. "Do you think having sex with a boy would help you do that?" More silence. "When we spoke the other day, you were talking about yourself, not Tiffany, weren't you?"

"Not exactly. Tiffany's always talking about it, how if you have a baby you can go on welfare, and they find you an apartment and give you money."

"Tiffany has a lot to learn, but even if that were true, it wouldn't really solve your problem. It would just add another one. It's not only unfair to use a baby to try to solve your own problems, but it wouldn't work. Instead of no longer having a mother to worry you once in a while, you'd have a baby to care for and worry about twenty-four hours a day."

She looked up at me, as if this was finally beginning to make sense.

"What you need is independence, and you can't get it that way. You need to finish school, and go to college."

"But I have four years of high school first." She frowned and clenched her fists in her lap.

I put my hand on hers. "There are other ways. What about your father?"

"I told you. He's married again and has a couple of other children."

"Does he keep in touch with you?"

"Sort of. He sends me birthday and Christmas

presents."

"Would he let you live with him, or visit for a while?"

She shrugged. "Maybe."

I warmed to the idea. "That would be ideal. How old are his new children?"

"Little. One's still a baby."

"Even better. If you lived there, you'd not only be away from your mother and get closer to your father, but you'd find out what it's like to take care of a baby day after day. Sort of a trial run."

"I'd like that, but maybe they wouldn't want me to live with them all the time."

"Perhaps you could just visit during school vacations."

"I guess I could ask."

I hugged her. "See, the future isn't so bleak after all."

"But what if nothing works? What if my mother won't get counseling? What if my father won't let me live with him even for a summer?"

"You have to try. Even if that doesn't happen, having a baby of your own is not the solution. It would just be one more problem you're not equipped to handle at your age." I turned her toward me and looked earnestly into her eyes.

"Kimberly, you're a very smart girl. And strong. All you have to do is go to school and get good grades so you can go to college, maybe go to a far-away college. If college doesn't work out, then learn some skills you can use to support yourself. Get a career. That way you'll be independent of everyone."

"Is that what you did?"

"In a way. I had a loving family to live with, but I did go away to college. It's only natural to want to be independent. So now I have a job and my own apartment and a car that the bank and I own together."

My little joke was rewarded with a smile.

"And no baby. You know it takes two people to make a baby, and you know what it's like to grow up without the father who was part of it. Don't do that to someone else. Wait until you and a man you love get married and can afford to start a family."

We hugged again and then I gave her one of my business cards. "Here. If you ever need to talk, you can call me. This is an eight-hundred number so it won't cost you anything. And if I'm not there, leave a message and I'll call you back just as soon as I can."

She took the card. "I know we're leaving tomorrow, but can we talk some more later?"

"I'm sorry. I'm leaving today." I looked at my watch. "Right now, in fact. I came down to the lobby to check out." I stood.

Kimberly rose as well and we hugged again. "Thanks," she gave me a weak smile and walked off.

I wondered if I should stay that last day so I could comfort Kimberly again if she needed it, but what was one more day? Besides, I doubted very much that Karen would complete the tour either after what had happened. In addition, I had another problem to solve, a problem that I hoped waited in Lake Como.

Chapter 22

I stepped off the bus in front of The Grand Imperiale Hotel, but, instead of going inside immediately, I let the bus drive off, turned around and admired the arm of Lake Como spread out before me. Although late afternoon by then, some sun still shone on the houses, churches, and hotels edging the blue water or nestled among trees climbing the mountains surrounding the lake. I could easily understand why it had become the quintessential vacation site for ancient Romans as well as other Europeans since ancient times.

Although its beauty impressed me, I remembered what had brought me on that mission. After the breakfast meeting which revealed the truth about Taylor, and my talk with Kimberly, I felt I had no choice but to go there. A water taxi took me to the station, a train sped me to Milan, and then a local bus brought me to Cernobbio, one of the many towns and villages that fringed the lake. That was the easy part. Next I had to find Taylor and explain what had happened. It suddenly occurred to me that perhaps Taylor had not come there after all, that perhaps my all-too-frequent impetuosity had made it a wild-goose chase. Excuse the cliché. The computer in my brain was experiencing overload.

The Grand Imperiale was a five-story white building with apple-green shutters at the windows and white wrought-iron railings across balconies. I picked up the handle of my suitcase and wheeled it toward the wide glass doors, my heart rocketing inside at the prospect of seeing, or maybe not-seeing Taylor.

Automatic doors swung open, and I pulled my suitcase across the red carpet toward the front desk. "Is a Mr. Taylor Mitchell registered here?"

After hitting a few keys and examining his computer screen, the clerk responded in perfect English. "Yes, madam, Mr. Mitchell is a guest. If you would like to ring his room, you may use a house telephone in the lobby." He pointed to several along the wall.

"No, thank you. I believe I'll check in first, that is, if you have a room available."

He consulted his computer some more, finally admitting they could accommodate me.

That done, I took the elevator to the fourth floor and found my room, small but elegantly appointed, with a queen-sized bed, chest of drawers, and a round table flanked by two overstuffed chairs. Long French windows opened to a tiny balcony edged in white wrought iron and a view of the lake over the rooftops of part of the hotel and outdoor restaurant.

I debated calling Taylor's room, but decided I didn't want to speak to him on the phone. I wanted to see him in person. But how? Where? I also didn't want to just appear on his doorstep. Besides, maybe he wasn't even in his room. He might be out taking pictures that he'd turn into paintings when he returned home. Perhaps I could see him at dinner. He'd have to eat sometime, and I could hang out in or near the hotel dining room until he showed up.

After unpacking and changing from my travel outfit into a silk blouse and matching pants, I put my sweater over my shoulders and returned to the first floor, where I spied a lounge and doors leading to a spacious dining room. Of course, it being Italy, the dining room didn't open until eight.

I scanned the few people sitting in the lounge, but none was Taylor. I debated staying there to wait for him to appear, but I was too restless and anxious. My mind reeled with the words I wanted to say to him, and then I rejected them as being sophomoric. I must have looked like a fool, mouthing speeches and frowning at nothing. I needed to wait somewhere else. I'd come back later, when the dining room opened.

I walked out onto a flagstone path, and the beautiful grounds made me forget for a moment what I'd come to do. I passed a bathhouse with an exercise room and finally a large lake-side swimming pool which was empty of swimmers. I returned to the flagstone walk, turned left and crossed the narrow street. I entered a small park with a dock and an ancient-looking stone bench. I saw a sign, printed in both Italian and French, and, since I remembered a little French, I read that boats picked up and deposited passengers who wanted to cross the lake.

The scene was so lovely, I wished I had my camera so I could take a picture. To my left, an ancient building rose from the water's edge, with stone steps descending from it and a tiny, weather-beaten wooden boat tied to a protruding post. I wanted to capture that on film as well.

That's when I saw him. He stood near the water, staring down, his hair tousled by a breeze that wafted across the lake.

"Taylor."

He whirled around and looked at me, and his face flushed with surprise. Or embarrassment. "What are you doing here?"

"I came to tell you that Karen Vale admitted she lied. Everyone knows the truth now." There, I'd said it already. After all my attempts at rehearsals, the simple words just tumbled out.

He took his time about acknowledging my statement. I waited what seemed like an eternity, wondering how he would react. He should be happy, but he didn't seem to be. A frown still creased his forehead.

Finally he closed the distance between us. "Thank you. Actually I hoped you'd come." He took my sweater from my arms and placed it around my shoulders as if nothing had happened since the last time we spoke. "It's getting chilly. I didn't *expect* you to come, of course. I just had a wild fantasy that you would."

I smiled at him. "Not so wild, as it turns out."

He took my hand, and we walked to the red brick sidewalk that edged the street, then turned right and followed it past a stone wall fronted by lilac bushes and tiny shops beginning to close for the night.

"Why did you leave Venice? Why didn't you wait until the, er, the mistake was cleared up? You should have known it would be."

He posed his own question. "Why did *you* leave the tour? What about your assignment? What about your job?"

"I got all the information I need for my article a

long time ago." I took a deep breath, eager to tell him what happened after he left. "I had to come. Not just because of... of us. I wanted you to know that Karen Vale admitted she lied and she knows you didn't abuse Kimberly."

"Then why did she say it?"

"You remember she was ill the day before? Well, she blames the medication she took for making her, um, a little crazy, I guess." I didn't voice Lance's suspicion she might have been drunk at the time.

Taylor stopped walking and turned to face me. "She admitted the truth to everyone?"

"Not exactly. She told Enza to do it. And Kimberly."

"She put that child through hell. The woman has no right to be a mother."

I touched his arm. "It's all over now. You can forget it."

"Forget it? Forget that she humiliated me in a crowded restaurant?" He thrust his hands deep in his pockets and walked some more, taking long, purposeful strides, as if his mind were elsewhere than on the narrow Italian street. I almost had to run to keep up with him.

He stopped walking suddenly and looked around, as if just realizing we'd gone rather far. "Let's go back."

Without waiting for my answer, he steered me across the street. We had passed a small restaurant before, but that time, glancing toward the dining room that could be seen through large plate-glass windows, he stopped. "Do you want to eat dinner?"

I felt queasy again. "I don't think I could eat just now."

Taylor led me inside anyway. "You need to whether you think so or not. Besides this one's open."

We sat in the corner booth of a charming room with subdued lighting, while on a glassed-in porch beyond, several tables of diners ate, smoked and talked. We both ordered the special dinner, but I barely touched mine, and I noticed Taylor ate almost none of his.

We didn't talk about what I was sure filled both our minds. I asked about Lake Como, and he told me more about what he'd learned from his previous visits.

"In a way I wish you hadn't come. I fantasized about taking you on a boat ride along the lake and we'd stop at every little village and explore everything. Then we'd climb up some of the steps carved into the hills and look down on it." He lowered his gaze. "But now we can't."

I felt a pain start in my midriff. "Why can't we? That sounds wonderful."

"You can't stay. You're supposed to be back home tomorrow. Your boss will fire you."

"I don't care. You know I'd rather be with you." He'd talked about my job, not about us. How could I tell him I wanted to stay when he seemed reluctant to continue our relationship? And he sounded so, well, normal. A short time before he'd been furious about Karen, and then he acted as if he didn't care. He seemed anxious for me to leave.

As usual, I spoke my mind. "It's no use pretending everything is fine with you when I know it isn't."

At that moment the waiter brought the dessert that was included in our meal, and, in spite of it being chocolate and my having a sweet tooth the size of Belgium, I refused it.

Taylor rose from the table and took the bill to the cashier, and I followed silently. I swallowed all the words I wanted to say until we were no longer surrounded by people.

As we walked back to the hotel, I decided not to talk about our having admitted our feelings to one another, about how close we'd come to making love, and the fact I still wanted him. Instead, I reminded him he needed to face what had happened with Karen and deal with it. "You can't just brush that aside."

His voice was a low growl. "Forgive and forget, is that it?"

"I'm sure you'll never forget, but you can forgive."

"Is that what you'd like me to do?"

I didn't want to push too hard. I hedged. "You've been seeing a counselor. You know he would tell you to forgive her. Maybe she didn't realize what she was doing."

"Oh, Karen Vale knew what she was doing all right."

"You mustn't let this make you bitter."

"I have a right to be bitter. I've been bitter for a long time, and nothing is going to change that."

We reached the hotel entrance, and he walked me through the lobby toward the elevators. "This isn't the first time, you know. First my parents refused to believe that I wasn't the father of Sally's baby. Now Karen—and everybody—thought I molested a child. What do they think I am, some kind of monster?"

Of course the truth was just the opposite. Taylor

was the most sensitive, caring man I'd ever met. That was why I loved him. "No, they don't. Even before Karen admitted she lied, everyone else believed you were innocent. They told me so."

That wasn't strictly the truth, but close enough.

I refused to give up. "Why have you never told your parents the truth about the baby? You should have cleared that up a long time ago. You could have found the girl and the child, had DNA testing and presented the proof."

"I couldn't."

"Of course you could."

"I did find Sally, but she told me the baby was stillborn."

"Oh, I'm so sorry."

"Under the circumstances, Sally was glad about it. She never needed to tell her mother that she was pregnant with her step-father's child."

"So you kept in touch with her. Do you know where she is now?"

"She changed her name to Fiona Blackwell, and she's doing fairly well as an actress in Hollywood."

"But even so, you must forgive your parents for their part in the misunderstanding. You said yourself you can't live the rest of your life with this between you."

The elevator doors opened and I stepped inside, but Taylor didn't enter with me. Just before the doors closed, he put his hand out to stop them. "Go home, Sydney. Don't tell me how I should feel when you, yourself have never forgiven the man who killed your brother."

He pulled back his hand and the doors closed between us.

* * *

I spent another restless night, rehashing in my mind everything we'd said, and especially Taylor's last words. He was right. I still harbored my own bitterness and had no right to accuse Taylor. I remembered how I had forgiven the local politician who chased me around the hotel room in Los Angeles only a few weeks before. Why not the man who killed my brother? What was different, except, perhaps, that the stakes were higher?

I found it harder to bear the knowledge that I had fallen in love with Taylor, and now we would never meet again. Tears rolled down my cheeks and soaked my pillow.

* * *

In the morning, I took the bus back to Milan and found a ticket office where I could verify my return flight to Los Angeles. As if in a dream, I caught a taxi to take me to Malpensa Airport. At the terminal. I checked in at the gate, discovered I had a short wait before my flight and used the time to sit in the waiting area and think about all that had happened. I knew I loved Taylor and decided to write a letter to him, even if he never received it. I remembered reading a book titled, *Letters to my Husband*, by a woman whose husband had died. Writing the letters made her feel close to him and eased her grief, and I needed that.

In the letter I told Taylor how I felt, how he was right that the hatred I'd harbored toward the man who killed my brother needed to be replaced by the very forgiveness I was asking from him. I wrote that I felt certain that Taylor, too, could find peace and forgiveness. I addressed it to him at the Grand Imperiale and hoped he would still be there when it arrived, or, if not, that the hotel would forward it to him. Wherever he'd gone. Here I was, in love with a man, and hadn't even managed to get his home address.

Nevertheess, I felt a comforting assurance in knowing that—even if we never met again—his own hatred would somehow be healed and he could embrace life again.

I boarded my flight and tried to immerse myself in the inflight movie. I even slept a little bit, no doubt catching up on what I'd missed the previous two nights. Thankfully, I had no seat mate to remind me of Taylor.

Chapter 23

So there I was in my office back home in Los Angeles on Monday morning, trying to return to a previous life as a reporter before I fell in love and had my heart broken. I also suffered from jet lag, but was intent upon trying to impress Mr. Hardcastle with my dedication. With no other future in sight, I really needed to keep my job. To say nothing of repaying student loans which only die when you do.

"Office" is really too fancy a word for the cubicle I occupied on the twenty-third floor of a steel and glass downtown building. True, I had my own desk and chair, plus a computer and printer, but there was no door, only an opening. Plus, the walls didn't come anywhere near the distant ceiling with its battery of fluorescent lights. They were nothing but moveable partitions and I could stand up and almost see over them. Yet, considering how difficult it was to find jobs in publishing, I considered myself lucky.

And then, at barely nine o'clock, Mr. Hardcastle himself came in, all two hundred plus pounds of him. My office held only the one chair, but, although I popped up so he could use it, he didn't sit. He spoke quickly, as if on the way to something way more important than seeing me.

"You're back," he mumbled.

"Yes, sir." I didn't add that was fairly obvious.

People state the obvious all the time.

He frowned and smoothed his gray comb-over. "When will you have the article ready?"

"Tomorrow?" I made it a question because I didn't know if I could really do justice to the subject by then.

"Take your time. Wednesday morning will be fine."

The man was all heart.

"About Italy," he said next. "I'm told you took an unauthorized side trip to Lake Como."

Hardcastle was a hands-on type of boss and, furthermore, there was apparently a tattle-tale in our midst.

"Um, yes." I didn't speak for a moment, having no idea how to explain my going there. "To talk to a man I fell in love with," lacked the proper respect for my assignment, and I wasn't about to tell him the whole magical—although ending rather badly—story.

"Well?" he prompted.

"Have you considered the possibility..." While my throat choked up, and tears gathered behind my eyelids, I scrambled to think of something plausible. "I mean, it's true the tour I was on didn't include Lake Como, but I heard that it's a world-wide tourist destination, and I couldn't resist seeing for myself. I'd like to do an additional article on it." I almost managed an encouraging smile. "Two stories for the price of one."

That was not totally impossible. True, I had never taken any pictures of my own, but, while buying a stamp to mail my letter to Taylor, I ran across a large picture book of Lake Como and bought it. That, plus what I had seen of it myself and Taylor's comments, should be enough for a short article.

Hardcastle made a "hmmm" sound, and rubbed his chin. "Have you turned in your expenses?"

"I'll have that ready this afternoon."

"I'll look it over and we'll talk. But don't count your chickens before they're hatched." He left, and I slumped into my chair.

I stared at the black face of my computer for several minutes. How could I write an article about a place and time where I'd met the man I wanted to spend the rest of my life with but couldn't? The memories crammed into those eleven days overwhelmed me.

I reminded myself life, indeed, goes on. I'd survived the death of my brother, and, somehow I'd survive this too. I took a deep breath, pulled out my notes, arranged the photographs from the tour company across my desk, and started to type. By the time I got to Venice—figuratively that is, and in my vision of what happened there—tears were running down my face and threatening to drown the keyboard. I gave up and took a long lunch hour. Or two.

Long ago I learned panic is an underrated component of writing to deadlines, and by afternoon I made a concerted effort to let professionalism rule. I put Taylor out of my thoughts and turned in my expense account. Then I wrote about the sights on the tour, not the people I shared them with. Grateful to have a first draft of the article completed, I left the office at five, went home and planned to collapse in bed. With luck, I'd be able to finish the job the next day and turn it in on Wednesday. That ought to please Hardcastle, and maybe he'd approve my expenses, including the trip to Lake Como. If I had to return that portion, my bank account would plunge to the low two figures, a territory that meant Tuna Helper for dinner several nights in a row.

At least I had something pleasant to look forward to at home, home being the apartment I shared with Nora. Since I'd returned—with an assist from Super Shuttle—very late on Sunday and had bee-lined it to the office that morning, we hadn't seen each other for more than two weeks.

She was in the kitchen stirring something delicious-smelling in a large pot on the stove, and when she heard me come in, she dropped her spoon and hugged me. "Are you glad to be back?" We broke apart, and she went back to tending the pot.

"Of course. You know what they say, 'Travel is wonderful, but home is where your clean clothes are.'"

She laughed. "Remember, I did warn you about taking only one suitcase. Ten days with the same people requires a whole lot more wardrobe than you packed."

"I really managed pretty well." I mentally pictured my luggage. "I couldn't have dragged another bag with me, not with the laptop, my purse and a tote for emergency supplies."

She pushed me gently toward a kitchen chair. "Sit here and tell me all about it. I've made a pot of minestrone—" She stopped and giggled before continuing. "—just in case you didn't get enough Italian food, and the garlic bread will be hot in a minute. Plus I made a lemon meringue pie."

"You're not supposed to feed me." I argued with her from the designated chair. "When we moved in together we decided to cook separately, remember? I recall you saying that you believed roommates often split up over food expenses, and you didn't want that to happen to us."

She smiled. "This is a special occasion. After all, you made a big fuss over my birthday. Besides it's only soup. I didn't make a Beef Wellington or Crepes Suzette."

But she could.

"What I served for your birthday party was all from Costco. You know I can't cook." Cook? I called my efforts *Cordon Noir* because I burned so many dishes.

On the other hand, Nora was not only a great cook, but a fantastic roommate in every other way. And a pleasure to be with. We actually met through the classified ad I placed, but she always seemed like the perfect girlfriend, someone I might have known since kindergarten, or shared a dorm room with in college. She was also beautiful, with her perfect figure, long blonde hair and Elizabeth Taylor eyes. She could have married any number of guys who hung around her, but she claimed she was in no hurry. A schoolteacher who loved her job, she wanted children, and too many guys she dated seemed cold to the idea of a family with a minimum of three boys and three girls. Really.

After putting two steaming bowls of soup on the already-set table, she sat down opposite me and repeated her invitation. "Tell me all about Rome."

"It's beautiful." I closed my eyes briefly, the better to visualize it. "And so is Florence. And Venice is indescribable. You have to see it to believe it."

Nevertheless, for the next hour, I did my best to describe everything I saw and everything I did and yet keep Taylor out of it. "You really ought to go to Italy.

Everybody should. It is absolutely wonderful, the food is divine, and the people are friendly. What more could you want?"

Nora removed our plates and brought out the pie. "You sound as if you'd like to live there."

"No, but I'd like to go back again. As a matter of fact, I might be able to do that, if I can get Mr. Hardcastle to agree with me on an article about Lake Como."

"Lake Como? I didn't think that was on your itinerary."

"It wasn't, but I went there anyway, and it's so lovely."

I stopped. So far I hadn't mentioned any of the people on the tour, although I had pointed out how Enza saw to our every need or wish, rather like a zealous den-mother.

"So why did you go to Lake Como?" Nora insisted.

I hesitated. Telling her why necessitated mentioning Taylor, to say nothing of Karen and Kimberly, a very long story, and an unpleasant one at that.

However, Nora wouldn't take no for an answer. "We'll have the pie and coffee in the living room, and you'll tell me everything." She stood and looked meaningfully into my eyes. "And I mean everything. I smell a romance here."

So we settled into the sofa and I spilled it all out.

"Oh, Sydney," she said when I finished the long story, "that's so sad. That Karen woman sounds like a real villain. What about the daughter? Did she really tell her mother Taylor had molested her?"

"No, Kimberly is a very sweet child and actually

treated Taylor more like the father who wasn't there. Karen made up the story about Taylor's molesting Kim." I sighed. "I hate to sound immodest, but it became obvious that Taylor preferred my company to hers and she was jealous."

"How awful. So that's why she tried to ruin Taylor's life."

"I hope it's not as bad as all that. He knows that she recanted her story. As I said, I went to Lake Como to tell him what happened after he left."

"You're in love with him, aren't you?"

I got up so hurriedly, I almost spilled my coffee. "Of course not. We only just met." I walked across the room, shielding my face from her gaze, afraid I'd begin to cry at the thought I'd never see Taylor again.

Nora came forward and turned me around to face her. "I'm glad you met someone, and he sounds like a wonderful person, just right for you."

"It's all over," I wailed. "He's so upset about what happened, to say nothing of the problem with his parents."

"His parents? What happened with his parents?"

So I had to tell Nora that story as well. "I'm afraid he'll just climb deeper into his shell and won't ever contact me."

"You said you wrote him a letter from Milan."

"But I don't know if he got it. And even if he did, he'll probably just think of me as someone he met on vacation and will never see again."

"Maybe he wants to see you again. Men do fall in love, you know, and when they do, they don't let a little thing like living in different cities stop them."

"Oh, Nora, I appreciate your confidence, but I can't let myself think about anything coming out of that brief relationship."

"Can't, or won't?"

"What difference does it make? I've done all I could. I followed Taylor to Lake Como and sent him that letter. There's nothing more I can do."

She squeezed my hand. "Oh, knowing you, you'll think of something."

She picked up our empty plates and cups from the coffee table and took them into the kitchen. I followed and helped her put them in the dishwasher and tidy the room.

"Now," she said finally, "I expect you need some sleep. Why don't you go along to bed? I have some students' papers to look over before I crash."

I started from the room and then remembered something. "I'm sorry. We've spent the whole evening talking about me, and I never asked you what you've been doing while I was gone."

Frankly, I didn't expect to hear anything unusual. She taught school every day, and on weekends she dated the latest guy in her life, Mike something-or-other, who, I suspected, was good company but not marriage material.

"Oh, nothing special. Unless you count my getting married next month."

It took me a moment to absorb that bombshell, but finally I screamed, "Nora!" and grabbed and hugged her until she begged for mercy.

"It's very sudden, I know, and I hate to leave you in the lurch. Do you think you can find another roommate by the middle of June?"

I sat down on a kitchen chair to think. "You've been a great roommate. I'll never find anyone as compatible as you've been. So I think I'll look for a smaller apartment and just live on my own."

Nora sat down next to me. "I'll miss you."

I laughed. "No, you won't. You'll have a husband and those six kids."

"Well, not all at once. The kids I mean. But Mike is the first man who acted as if the whole idea didn't scare him to death."

"I like him," I said, not that it mattered, "and I think you two will make a great couple."

"She clutched my hand. "I have you to thank for this."

"Me? I didn't introduce you to him."

"No, but you influenced me."

"How? I'm not married, and prospects don't exactly look promising for the near future, so how could I influence you?"

"Your ideals influenced me. I liked the fact you hold yourself up to a high standard. I could have chosen to just live with Mike—he asked me lots of times—but I'd think of you and say, 'No, I need a real commitment. I don't want to just play house.'"

"So?"

"So he proposed." She grinned. "And I want you to be my maid of honor."

"I'd be honored." We hugged again.

As I went into my room and undressed for bed, the tears flowed again. Nora would marry her Mr. Right, and I would never get to marry mine. For her sake I'd have to do a better job in the future of hiding my feelings. I'd treat my breaking heart like a television set on Mute.

Chapter 24

Early the next morning, as we both headed to the kitchen for breakfast, I approached Nora. "I can't be your maid of honor."

Nora's eyes widened, and she gasped. "Why not?"

"Because I'd ruin your beautiful day, that's why."

"How could you ruin it?"

"Because, as you very well know, I'm a klutz and sometimes, well, sometimes things happen that aren't really my fault."

Nora laughed and patted my hand. "Nothing will happen."

I poured cereal into a bowl. "Almost five years ago I ruined my sister's wedding, so it's possible."

"And just how did you do that?"

I kept the story fairly short, telling her I was maid of honor that time too, but skipping over the details, like the beautiful chapel, the flowers, the music and my proud parents sitting together in the first row. I was going to omit the gorgeous dresses on bride and bridesmaids, but that was an important part of what happened.

"I was wearing this really beautiful long dress—"

Nora interrupted me. "I would have known your sister would choose beautiful dresses. Sometimes the bride chooses really dorky ones for the bridesmaids."

"These were lovely, with a plain bodice, short

puffed sleeves, wide satin sashes, and bouffant skirts that stood out like little tents."

"What color were they?" Nora wanted to know, as if already getting ideas for her own attendants.

"Pink, a lovely shade of pink."

"Go on. What happened?" She sat and stared at me.

I briefly recounted how, near the end of the ceremony, I handed my bouquet to the bridesmaid next to me and took the bride's bouquet. When the minister asked for the tokens of the union, the best man produced the ring for the bride, and her husband-to-be slipped it on her finger. Next the minister asked for the bride's token and, as I was holding that ring, I then committed my first *gaffe* of the day.

"What did you do that was so terrible?"

"I dropped it. Actually I didn't drop it right away. I had been afraid I would, so I put it on my own finger. Well, being a man's ring, it was too loose for my finger so I put it on my thumb, and then, when it was time to go on the groom's finger, it wouldn't come off."

"So how could you drop it?" Nora's lips curled into a grin.

"Well, they saw me struggling to pull it off. My fingers must have swollen during the ceremony. So the groom leaned over to help, and it finally came off in a rush, and it fell on the floor."

"You said you dropped it."

"To this day, I don't know who dropped it, but suddenly we were all stooping over to pick it up, and, my dress being so long and full, I accidentally stepped on the front of the skirt. After the groom retrieved the ring and gave it to my sister, I tried to straighten up, but my foot was caught in the dress, so I tripped and fell forward."

Nora's voice rose in shock. "You fell down?"

"Not totally. I fell on top of the minister, and he kept me from landing on the floor."

"But he fell down?"

"Partly, but he recovered very quickly, because the groom and all the attendants rushed over to help us."

Nora was laughing by then. "So there you all were huddled over at the altar like a well-groomed football team?"

I giggled. "Well, sort of, if you imagine half the team looking like penguins and the other half like lawn flamingos." I remembered something else. "Some bouquets got crushed in the process and there were flower petals everywhere."

After we caught our breaths, I shrugged. "So you see what I mean. You don't want me to ruin your wedding. I'll be a bridesmaid, but don't give me anything important to do."

Nora wiped her eyes. "But it's so funny. Didn't anyone laugh?"

"Oh, yes, everyone laughed, even the minister. When we were all standing up again, he said, 'Will the photographer please erase the last thirty seconds from the tape?'"

Nora chuckled some more. "And then?"

"And then, after the guests stopped laughing, he went on with the ceremony as if nothing had happened." I smiled, remembering. "Except for an occasional grimace he made trying to repeat his lines, and the bridesmaid on my left giggling into the flowers in what was left of her bouquet."

"I wouldn't call that ruining the wedding, and I'll bet your sister doesn't think you did, either."

"She's my sister. Of course she had to forgive me."

"Well, don't think that story lets you off the hook. You're my maid of honor, like it or not."

* * *

Nora's wedding the next month was lovely, and I didn't do anything wrong. Actually, the wedding was more lavish than I expected, at a fancy hotel overlooking the Pacific Ocean. It was held outdoors on a grassy bluff above the beach, with arbors of flowers and white chairs festooned with ribbons for the hundred or more guests.

While I helped Nora into her designer dress before the ceremony, I learned that her parents were loaded. They were in fact, as I learned that day, her adoptive parents.

"Am I not the luckiest woman in the world?" she said. "I've had the most wonderful life, and now I'm having the most beautiful wedding."

I thought of something. "If your family has so much money, how come you wanted to move in with me and share the rent?"

"Well, I'm only a schoolteacher. Sure my parents could have paid the rent on an apartment for me, but I wanted to be independent. I wanted to do it on my own, like other people have to do."

"Besides," she added, "I was an only child, and I liked the idea of having a roommate, sort of like the sister I always wished I had. It gave me a chance to meet you, and I'm grateful for that. You know I think of you like a sister, and we'll always be best friends, won't we?"

"Of course." I hugged her, but my curiosity got the better of me. "Did you ever meet your birth mother?"

She sat down on one of the chairs in the dressing room. "Yes, actually I did once. One year it seemed as if every newspaper and magazine ran an article about people doing that, so I did it too."

"And what happened? Did you like her?"

"She seemed like a very nice person, but she had no interest in having a relationship with me."

I frowned. "Didn't that upset you?"

"No." She leaned close and spoke softly. "Listen, I don't know how other people handle these things, but in our case, it was the right thing. I met her at a coffee shop because she didn't want us to meet at either her house or mine. She said she was only fifteen when she got pregnant with me and knew she was too young to have a child and could never support me. So she gave me up for adoption the instant I was born."

Pregnant at fifteen reminded me of Kimberly's friend Tiffany who was fifteen and wanted a baby.

"She told me," Nora said, "that she knew my adoptive parents would always be my real parents because they'd raise me from birth, and she simply closed that chapter of her life."

"But how did that make you feel?"

She paused and then smiled. "Like she was the most unselfish mother in the world. She must have loved me very much because she gave me up so I could have what she knew she could never give me herself—a wonderful set of parents who not only had lots of money, but lavished all their time and attention on me. By doing that, she blessed me in a thousand ways, and I told her how grateful I was to be able to say 'thank you' in person."

So you can understand we were both a little teary-eyed when someone knocked on the door and said it was time to start the wedding. During the ceremony I had nothing to do but hold a bouquet of flowers, and I did it expertly. Afterward, pictures were taken and then we all went indoors. The reception featured unlimited hors d'oeuvres and punch, a five-course meal served at tables with enormous flower centerpieces and satin-covered chairs, a live band with musicians dressed in tuxedos, and a wedding cake large enough to feed a small African nation.

* * *

Nora insisted on paying her share of the rent on our apartment through the end of the month, but I dreaded the prospect of finding a smaller one. No way could I afford the two bedrooms that Nora and I occupied. I, too, loved my roommate like a sister and was happy she was married, but I wondered how I could cope with the change in my life.

Nevertheless, one morning a week after the wedding I awoke with a better attitude. Looking for a new apartment would be a challenge that would take my mind off Nora on her fabulous honeymoon and my losing Taylor. Yeah, right.

Taylor was never far from my thoughts. I remembered every moment we spent together, the look on his face when he told me he might be falling in love with me, the feel of his arms around me in the gondola, the taste of his mouth on mine. My body ached with longing to touch him, hold him. I cried myself to sleep Monday, Tuesday, Wednesday... well, you get the picture.

* * *

The idea came to me over the next weekend. I had found a one-bedroom apartment that seemed suitable. It not only boasted a modern kitchen, but was on the first floor and had a little garden in back. The landlord told me it had been occupied for a long time by a woman who moved up to a house in Beverly Hills thanks to writing a screenplay that became a feature film.

I loved hearing that, because every writer in Los Angeles—to say nothing of every secretary, pool boy and parking lot attendant—dreams of writing a successful movie script. In fact, I don't deny it was on my own list of "Things to do before I'm forty."

So the idea I dreamed up came to me as a result of thinking about that woman's having made it. Plus I remembered Taylor saying that the girl from his home town who had been pregnant—but not by him—had moved to Hollywood, changed her name and was now a successful film actress.

What if, I said to myself, I went to see her and she would agree to visit Taylor's parents and tell them the truth? Then perhaps they'd contact him and the stalemate would be over.

Okay, what happened between Taylor and his parents was none of my business, but I couldn't help it. He might not love me, but I was still in love with him, and I would do anything for him. Besides, when I see a way to fix a problem, I just want to get busy and do it.

Not only that, it looked so easy. First, I knew her name. Second, she worked in Hollywood, only minutes away from my own job. Third, I could use my credentials as a magazine writer to interview her for a story. I didn't clear this with Hardcastle first, but it seemed to me he ought to approve an article about a local actress about to star in a film everyone anticipated.

Naturally he had a different plan for me. That week I was to go to the Getty Museum and write an article about their upcoming special exhibit.

"You did a good job on that foreign art in Rome," he said. "This should be right up your alley." In case you hadn't noticed, my boss never met a cliché he didn't like.

I calculated a day should be enough for that story, so I put it off temporarily and instead set the wheels in motion to find Fiona Blackwell and convince her to tell Taylor's parents he wasn't the father of her baby. Little Miss Fix-it, that's me.

Chapter 25

I started with the Screen Actors Guild, and it wasn't long before I was able to speak to Fiona's agent and arrange for an interview.

Unlike the screenwriter who had moved up to Beverly Hills, Fiona occupied an apartment in town. A uniformed doorman hovered in front of the building, and, once inside the lobby, he made me show him my press pass and I.D. before he'd even call upstairs to verify I was expected. In addition, the elevator, although presumably a do-it-yourself modern apparatus, required an operator in uniform. He was a handsome boy who looked not a day over twelve, but, judging by his height, was probably sixteen and would be a movie star by twenty-one.

At her door, Fiona herself let me in, and I found myself in the presence of a beautiful woman with blonde hair, enormous blue eyes and a figure I'd never achieve even if I gave up chocolate for a year. She wore a fuchsia silk blouse and plum-colored silk pants, a patterned scarf at her neck and fancy sandals on bare feet whose toenails, no doubt painted by some lackey at a salon I could never afford, coordinated with her color scheme.

"Come in." She gave me a broad smile. "You may not believe it, but I read *L. A. Life.*"

"I'm so pleased."

"Do sit down." She ushered me to a set of low

couches that faced windows with a great view, but I sat instead in a straight upholstered chair with my back to all that light. She took her place on one of the sofas and spread her arms along the back, seemingly totally at ease.

Then, all business, I pulled out my notebook and asked the questions any reporter would begin with. Like, where was she born, and how did she happen to get into show business?

She named Chicago as her home town, admitted her father died when she was young, but never said her mother married again or that she ran away from home after high school. She said she was always interested in acting and appeared in high school and college plays.

"What college did you attend?"

She didn't hesitate. She'd been interviewed many times before, no doubt, and had her answers prepared. "Right here in California, but that was before I changed my name."

I filled in the short silence that followed. "So you mean I can't check that out?"

"Do you want to?"

"Well, your college acting experience undoubtedly helped you get a start in films, so it's not a secret."

She rose and walked to a corner cabinet and poured a glass of water from a decanter. "Would you like a drink, or some water?"

"No, thank you."

"My publicist has a handout with all that stuff about my early years. I assumed you wanted to talk about my upcoming film." After giving me a printed biographical sketch, she returned to her seat.

I glanced at the paper quickly and tucked it under

my notebook in my lap. I had done my homework and knew the name of her upcoming film, so we talked about that for a good twenty minutes.

She glanced at her diamond-studded watch. "Well, if there's nothing more—"

"Actually, I want to talk about something else, if you don't mind." I closed my notebook. "Strictly off the record."

She frowned. "I hope you're not going to ask me if I can get you in the movies."

Her question took me by surprise. "Why on earth would I do that?"

"You're very pretty. When you first came in, I thought you looked more like an actress than a reporter."

I may have blushed. "Thank you, but I have no such ambitions. I couldn't act my way out of a paper bag."

She smiled and seemed to relax. "Okay, what is it you want to know?"

"It's about an incident that happened a long time ago." I took a deep breath and plunged right in. "I met Taylor Mitchell recently, and he told me he knew you."

I paused to let her say something about their relationship, but instead she threw the conversational ball back to me. "How did you happen to meet Taylor?"

"On an airplane, actually. We were both going overseas and ended up on a tour of Rome, Florence and Venice."

"How nice. I expect he's become very successful then. I'm glad."

"As successful as he wants to be."

"Is he married? Does he have children?"

"No."

"If he's as handsome as he once was, I'm surprised." She took a sip of water, then seemed to have a sudden inspiration. "Oh, I know. You two fell in love on that tour, right?"

I hadn't seen that coming either, and had no ready response for it. "Not exactly. We did talk a lot, and he told me some things about his past."

Fiona shifted uneasily on the sofa. "I can't imagine why that should interest a reporter. He was an all-American kid from a nice family. No skeletons in their closet that I'm aware of."

Unlike her own, that was. Still, I needed to get to the point, so I kept going. "He told me that, when he was home from college for the summer and you were a high school senior named Sally, he helped you leave town."

Fiona, or Sally, was on her feet immediately and paced the floor. "He told you?" She whirled around toward me. "You can't print that. It isn't true."

"No, I'm not going to print it."

"Then why...?"

"He told me you were pregnant and were afraid to tell your mother that your stepfather had raped you." I rushed on. "You wanted to get away, and he gave you some money so you could do that."

She sat down again, rested her head on her arms and remained silent for a long time. Finally, as if making a decision, she looked up and leaned toward me. I sensed her tears were close to the surface.

"I try not to think about it. Mostly, it's more like a

movie I watched than anything that actually happened to me." She looked up. "I'd like to keep it that way, please."

"I'm sorry to bring up a painful chapter in your life. I wouldn't ask you to remember it if it wasn't important."

"Important to you? How?"

"No, of course not. I mean to Taylor."

She tilted her head back. "I'll never forget his kindness."

I didn't comment, and she continued. "I wanted to hide in a big city, so I came to Los Angeles and got a job as a waitress. But as my pregnancy progressed, I finally had to quit working. Taylor's money kept me alive for those last three months."

"And then?" I already knew what happened next, but I wanted to hear her version.

"The baby was stillborn." She searched vainly for a handkerchief in her pockets, then put the edge of her scarf up to her eyes for a moment. "Just as well. I was going to give it up for adoption anyway."

"Taylor told me he knew what happened to the baby. I guess you two kept in touch."

"For a while we did, and then, well, you know how that is. People get busy, and sometimes they move." She looked up, now seeming more comfortable talking to me. "So you saw Taylor on the tour. Was that recently? He's okay?"

"Not quite. He's doing well financially. He started a software business in college. Perhaps he told you about that, and he sold it a few years ago. Besides that income, he's an artist and a computer consultant and seems to enjoy both of those occupations."

"I'm so happy for him." She got up again and refilled her glass of water. "I'll never be able to thank him enough for what he did."

"Well, at the time, I guess he had some savings he was able to give you."

She turned and sat down again. "Oh, it was much more than that." After a pause, she looked questioningly at me. "He didn't tell you all of it, did he?"

"What do you mean? What more is there?"

"We lived next door to each other, and after I told him what had happened, he, um, he wanted to protect me." She hurried on. "There were still two more weeks of school, and I needed that diploma. Besides I had to make plans for how I'd get away." She took another swallow, and then spoke softly, as if afraid someone else might hear. "Every night, after his parents went to bed, he came over, and I let him in my bedroom window."

My voice rose in shock. "He what?"

"No, you don't understand. He didn't touch me. He slept on the floor in a sleeping bag right in front of my door so my stepfather couldn't..." She shivered and crossed her arms. "I'd set my alarm, and he'd leave early in the morning."

"So he kept you safe. Did your stepfather ever try to..."

"I don't know for sure. I never heard him try to get in, and Taylor never said anything."

My mind reeled with that new information. Taylor had slept in her room to keep her stepfather from raping her again. He might have been seen going back and forth from her house. No wonder rumors flew. Perhaps his parents found out where he was going, and it gave them even more reason to doubt his claims of innocence. My mouth turned dry as an old tennis ball.

"Thank you." I licked my lips. "I think I will have that glass of water now."

While she poured the water, I rose and did some floor-pacing of my own. My mission was all the more urgent then. I sat on the sofa next to her.

"You really feel indebted to Taylor, don't you?"

"Of course. I'd do anything for him."

"Well, I know just what 'anything' is."

She frowned as if I were going to ask her to shoot someone or, maybe worse, denounce her show business career and go into a convent.

"I want you to tell this story to someone else."

She shook her head slowly from side to side. "I know movie stars get away with lots of weird behavior these days, but I'm not that famous, and it could just ruin my career."

"This is very important."

"You don't understand. Even if I were willing to risk it, there are my parents to consider. They're still alive. In fact, my mother still lives with my stepfather. I can't make this story public. I don't care what happens to him, but it would probably kill her."

"I don't want you to broadcast it to the world. Only to Taylor's parents."

"Why?"

"Because after you left town, rumors began to fly that you were pregnant and Taylor was the father."

She paused as if considering that for the first time. "Yes, I suppose they would think that."

"Taylor's parents think so, and they never believed him when he said he wasn't." I took another gulp of water before continuing. "You see, he was their only child, and they believed that, by his giving you the money to run away, he deprived them of knowing their grandchild."

"But he wasn't the father. Didn't he tell them?"

"He tried, but, when the baby died, he couldn't even get DNA evidence to prove it."

"Oh, dear. I never thought of that. I've been so selfish, and never realized what might have happened to Taylor. He seemed so, so capable and strong and wise."

"Also stubborn," I added. "He was so angry when his parents refused to believe him, even without any proof, that he just left home and never went back."

She looked truly upset. "I'm so sorry."

"He won't forgive them for their lack of faith in him. They don't even know the baby died, because he was long gone by then."

"That's so awful."

"What happened to you was awful too, but you were both very young then and did what seemed right at the time. I really think you need to help Taylor now, though."

"I'd like to, but I don't know if I can."

"You know where his parents lived. You can go there. You're the only one who can tell them the truth about what really happened."

She stood up and took a deep breath. "I remember Taylor's parents. Like my own, his mother was older when she gave birth to him, and I guess she felt, having that in common, they could be friends. But my stepfather always interfered. He didn't want my mother to have friends. Instead, he isolated her from other people. Me too."

"Yet he let you go to school."

"If it hadn't been the law, he might not have." She frowned, as if remembering those days caused a lot of pain. "I was only allowed to go to school and occasionally to the store for groceries." She looked up. "That's how I met Taylor. He worked at the store."

"He told me how you finally confided in him."

"He was so... I can't explain it. Somehow I just knew he could help me. And he did."

"When that happened, the two of you should have gone to the police and told them."

She put up a hand and shook her head. "I'm not trying to justify myself, but you don't know how traumatic it was. I only wanted to get away. I wanted to forget everything about those days, start a new life. And I didn't want to hurt my mother. I'm sure she didn't know what was happening, and, if it came out, the scandal would have killed her."

"She doesn't have to know. You have a new life, a very successful one. You've survived the past, but now you need to help Taylor survive the same past."

I got up and stood in front of her, waiting for her answer.

She stood too and took my hand in hers. "Of course I will."

"Do you remember the address where Taylor lived?"

"How could I forget? It was right next door to us." She moved to the desk and picked up a small calendar. "And if his parents aren't still living there, I think I can

track them down. Plus, there's always the Internet."
   I grinned and we high-fived each other.

Chapter 26

In some ways it seemed like a miracle that Fiona had agreed to help me. In addition, Hardcastle approved my expense account, so I didn't have to start eating the free food samples they give out at Costco. However, I didn't gloat over my successes. I still had another problem to solve.

My brother had been killed by a drunken driver almost two years before, but, thanks to a clogged court system and the defensive lawyers' continuances, the trial was just now ending. Because of my job, I couldn't go to the courtroom every day during the trial, although my parents and older brother went often, but I knew I had to be at the sentencing.

As I drove to the courthouse, I remembered that day in Milan. I sat in the waiting room writing the letter to Taylor and suddenly heard a voice in my head telling me that I must forgive the man who killed Howard. That, by doing so, I was not giving up something valuable. It didn't grant that man some reward he didn't deserve. He gained nothing from it. Refusing to forgive meant I held onto all the pain of the past myself.

Yes, the intervention by my family had enabled me to get on with my life, but the agony was always there, just below the surface. By not forgiving, I held onto my vision of a bad person, as well as my own self-pity. I was keeping myself from forgiving *me*.

Inside the courthouse, I hugged my parents and my brother Owen. He told me that Jennifer had decided not to come, but remained in Texas with her own family.

When we were called, we passed through wide double doors, and entered a large, wood-panelled room. I saw a judge in a black robe sitting above everyone behind a desk built into the back wall. I thought it looked just like those courtrooms in television programs, one thing Hollywood got right.

My mind focused on what I'd say, I hardly heard the proceedings. Finally, the defendant and his lawyer stood up, and the judge turned to us and asked if we had anything to say before he pronounced sentence.

My parents and brother spoke briefly, but I don't remember any of it. When I stood up, so far as I can recall, I said something like, "I know he didn't kill my brother intentionally. He used bad judgment and made a terrible mistake, but I don't hate him. I forgive him because I've learned that forgiveness is the right thing to do. Not just for his sake, but also for our own."

Fortunately I had nothing more to say, because tears welled in my eyes, and my knees were so wobbly I felt as if they were made of cooked linguini.

The judge thanked me, gave the man the minimum sentence and we all left the courtroom. In the corridor, the four of us hugged and cried and my father said, "You did the right thing." Then some reporters crowded around us, asking their dumb questions, like, "How did you feel...?"

* * *

I loved autumn. The weather could be counted on to be pleasant with warm days and balmy nights, and the tiny garden behind my apartment still produced roses, both pink and red, that I could cut and bring indoors. As I cut a rose on Saturday morning, I heard my doorbell ring, and put down my clippers to go inside to answer it.

I hoped it wasn't a sales person. After the "Do Not Call" list stopped telemarketers from trying to sell you something you didn't want over the phone, some companies decided to go back to house calls. I didn't mind the Avon ladies. After all, trying to stay youthful-looking is one of women's major avocations if not a downright necessity. However, I was in no mood for it that morning. Instead I opened the door to see Taylor Mitchell standing on my threshold. Talk about an answer to a prayer.

He looked tan and fit, wore a gray short-sleeved polo shirt and blue jeans and held a small package in his left hand which he kept at his side.

My heart threatened to jump right out of my chest, and I couldn't speak for a whole minute. Finally I stepped back from the open door to invite him in. "What a surprise." What a cliché. "It's been—"

"Almost six months," he finished for me. "And I thought of you every day."

My funny little heart did flip-flops. He came in, and I pointed to a chair. "Would you like some coffee or lemonade?"

"Nothing." He sat on the offered chair. "You look wonderful, every bit as beautiful as I remembered."

My cheeks burned. "You look good too, but how

did you find me?" I added quickly, "From the letter I sent you?"

"No, you forgot to put your return address on it. Enza helped. She knew how much you meant to me, and, after Karen Vale told those lies, she thought that getting your address for me was the least she could do."

I remembered losing my former apartment because of Nora's leaving to get married. "I'd moved."

"I know. The address Enza gave me was the old one, but it was a place to start, and people are incredibly easy to find these days."

"Aren't you supposed to be working somewhere, like Arizona?"

"Not really. I've been exhibiting my paintings at art shows during the summer, and I saved the last one for here in Los Angeles so I could come to see you."

Silence followed. Not knowing what to say next, I sat on the sofa.

"I'll start my new job next week." He paused and picked up the package he'd placed on the floor when he sat down. "I really meant it when I said I thought of you every day, so I accepted a job with a company here in L.A. where I could be close to you."

He wanted to be near me? The thought sent waves, some of them as big as tsunamis, crashing through my body.

"I have something for you." He leaned forward and extended the wrapped package.

I took it, removed the blue satin ribbon and shiny foil paper and opened the small box. Inside, swathed in tissue paper, lay a silver bracelet.

"I bought it in Florence." He grinned. "For you. I

just didn't know when I'd give it to you though."

"It's lovely, but I don't think I should accept it."

"It's a thank-you gift for what you did for me."

"I didn't do anything."

He chuckled, looked up, and then shook his head. "You did everything. Most of all, you wrote that wonderful letter."

"I worried that you wouldn't get it."

"I was still at the hotel in Cernobbio, so I got the letter and read it. You talked about how our conversation changed you, and I knew then that you would forgive the man who killed your brother. I reasoned that, if you could do it, then I could forgive too."

In spite of the tears that filled my eyes, I told him about the day in the courthouse, and how afterward I felt liberated from the pain of holding onto the past.

He nodded as if he understood. "Since coming home, all the time I made paintings from my photographs of Venice, I was trying to figure out why I was beginning to feel that way."

"What do you mean?"

"When I let go of self-righteousness, I finally realized that forgiving was a choice I could make. But I wanted to understand it logically, not just emotionally. Do you know what I mean?"

"I think so."

"I don't usually give long speeches, but I want you to understand, because you need to believe that I'm over the bitterness and anger."

"I think I believe it already." He did look calm and relaxed, at peace with the world.

"You see, I figured out that there are two elements to forgiveness. One is that you give up the resentment you're entitled to. I mean, I was entitled to resent my parents' treatment, as well as Karen's lying, wasn't I?"

"Well, it would be understandable."

"So you deliberately give that up."

"And you're okay with that?"

"I am now, and that's not all. The other element is that you give a gift to the person who hurt you, your compassion—your moral love—even though they might not deserve it." He grinned again, as if proud to have worked it out in his mind. "They don't have a right to your goodness, but you give it anyway."

"Because—" I prompted.

"Because they're human beings too." He stood up and paced the floor for a moment, his face animated, almost glowing. "Forgiveness gets a bad rap because people think you do all the giving and the other person does all the getting, but it isn't like that. It isn't about justice."

"You mean like 'n eye for an eye.'"

"Right. Forgiveness means you don't have to look at what the person did, but at who they are, people who, perhaps like many of us, are still learning how to live in the world. And you can forgive that person, even love them, not because of what they did, but in spite of it."

During the pause that followed, I marveled at his recitation. "So did you forgive Karen Vale?"

"Yes. I wrote a letter to her and said I forgave her, and Enza promised to forward it for me." He looked down for a moment. "While I was at it, I told Karen to be good to Kimberly."

"That's great."

He came to the sofa and sat close to me, taking my hand in his. "And there's more. You found Fiona and told her to visit my parents and tell them the truth."

"When did you find out about that?"

"Not for awhile. In fact, the wonderful thing is that I had decided to forgive my parents before I knew about it, before it happened, actually."

"You forgave them as well?"

"You'll never guess what happened. When she opened the door, my mother threw herself in my arms and kissed me. Before I could say a word, she and my dad both asked my forgiveness for not believing in me."

"How wonderful."

"And then, while I was still there that week visiting my folks, Sally, I mean Fiona, arrived and told them all about what happened years ago."

I felt more tears gather in my eyes. and I tightened my hold on his hand. "I'm so happy for you."

Taylor picked up the silver bracelet and put it in my hand again. "So you see, you deserve this."

"Not really."

"Okay, then, it's an engagement present."

I think the tsunami hit me, because I felt swamped.

He hurried on. "If you haven't fallen in love with anyone else since Lake Como, I want you to think about marrying me."

My heartbeat escalated, and warmth rushed through my veins, but I couldn't speak. My hand, holding the beautiful bracelet, trembled like the leaves that were falling from my solitary tree in the little garden outside.

Finally I managed to say, "I've thought of you every

day, too, but we really haven't known each other very long. Eleven days—" I stopped. Where had that come from? I loved this man.

"It was a start. We can see each other, date for a few months like people do."

I didn't need to hear any more. I just threw myself in his arms and kissed him.

When we finally broke apart, Taylor said, "I often thought I'm not worthy of you, and it's taken me awhile, but as you see, I finally, well, got it."

He leaned forward and kissed me again, then kissed my cheeks and my chin and even my nose. "My sweet Sydney, will you accept my gift and, at least, think about marrying me?"

I could only nod. Forgiveness had brought me more than peace. It would bring me a chance to love and be loved.

* * *

Taylor and I visited Fiona together to thank her for what she'd done.

She ushered us in and offered some Perrier. "I was glad to do it. It's not often a person gets to set things right. I feel like a character I played in a film." She giggled.

"What about your mother?" Taylor asked. "Does she know what really happened all those years ago? Will you ever tell her?"

"No, and thank goodness I don't have to." She poured some water for all of us and sat on the sofa next to me. "After I visited your parents, I decided it was time to visit my own. I didn't plan to tell her the truth, just see her and maybe tell her I loved her."

"What a great thing to do," I said. "She probably worried about you after you disappeared so long ago."

Fiona sighed. "I'll never know. She didn't recognize me."

"Because, now that you're an actress, you look different?" Taylor asked.

"No, because she has Alzheimers." She paused and a pained expression crossed her face. "She doesn't know anyone. My stepfather has to take care of her now."

Taylor's voice took on a hard edge. "Serves him right. I've heard about how difficult caring for a person with the disease can be. After what he did to you, that's at least a partial repayment."

"I forgave him." Fiona stood up. "I guess the mood was catching. After talking to you and your folks and everyone forgiving one another, I knew I had some forgiving to do myself." She walked toward the window and looked out. "He was a very selfish person, and he did a wicked thing."

"You're right." Fiona turned to us. "Show business gets a bad rap sometimes, but I've made wonderful friends. Besides," she added, "if that hadn't happened, if I hadn't met you and come to L.A., I might never have had this career."

Taylor stood and raised his glass of Perrier. "To good things happening to good people."

* * *

In case you were wondering, Kimberly wrote to me,

using the business address on the card I'd given her:

Dear Sydney (Miss Cooke):
I had to write and tell you what's happened. You were right about my father and stepmother being willing to have me visit them. I stayed the whole summer and had a great time. Dad's new wife is very nice, and the baby is adorable. You were right about that too. No way would I want to have a baby of my own at this time in my life. They need lots of attention, and I'm having way too much fun now.
And, guess what? When I got home, my mom, instead of being upset for my wanting to visit my dad, as I thought she might be, was nicer to me than ever. Maybe she missed me, you think?
So, thanks again for the advice. I guess older people really do know a few things.
Love, Kimberly.

I didn't care much for the "older people" label, but I was happy things had worked out so well for her.

As for Hardcastle, not only did he like my article about the Italian tour, he also liked the one I wrote about Fiona. Which was fortunate because I had completely forgotten I was supposed to do one on the Getty Museum, and by the time I remembered and got it written I was a week late turning it in. However, it was brilliant, if I do say so myself.

Plus, my suggestion of an article about Lake Como turned out to be inspired. Hardcastle called me into his office to discuss the assignment.

"Your preliminary article is fine, but a bit short for such a vast area. How soon can you do a longer one?"

I hesitated. "Well, that depends."

"The Italian tour story went over very well, and perhaps we should strike while the iron is hot, and do a comprehensive article about the entire Italian lake district as a follow-up."

"When?"

"I thought for next spring."

"Does that mean—?"

"Yes, I'm sending you to Lake Como on an expense account." He wagged a finger in my face. "And, Cooke, stay within the budget this time."

"Of course." Behind my back, I crossed my fingers.

Taylor's new job left him time to be with me every weekend and lots of evenings in between. When I told him what Hardcastle said, his face lit up, and he grinned as if he'd just discovered a cure for Internet spam.

"I have an idea." He put his arms around me and drew me so close I thought I could feel his heart beating under his shirt.

"What would that be?"

"I think your Lake Como assignment would make a grand excuse for a honeymoon."

I quite agree with him.

THE END

IF YOU LIKED THIS BOOK......

...visit the author's website and check out her other romance novels: **www.phyllishumphrey.com**

COLD APRIL - A love story set on the Titanic

FINDING AMY- Visiting England for her grandfather's funeral, a young Chicago businesswoman finds herself in the middle of intrigue and romance.

NORTH BY NORTHEAST – On a sightseeing train trip, a jewel heist and a kidnapping give a schoolteacher and a mysterious passenger more excitement than they bargained for.

ONCE MORE WITH FEELING – A female San Francisco stock broker deals with a handsome new client, his eccentric twin aunts and an insider trading scandal.

SOUTHERN STAR – Written with co-author Carolann Camillo, the novel takes the reader on a yacht trip in the Bahamas, where anything can happen. And does.

STRANGER IN PARADISE – The manager of a Hawaiian hotel is about to lose her job because of a handsome stranger. And then a tsunami strikes the island.

FREE FALL – Can a woman who's afraid of heights fall in love with a skydiver?